FIRST THINGS FIRST

How to effectively rearrange your life through the principle of First Fruits.

Paula White

FIRST THINGS FIRST

How to effectively rearrange your life through the principle of First Fruits.

Paula White

PUBLISHED BY PAULA WHITE ENTERPRISES - TAMPA, FLORIDA

First Things First
How to effectively rearrange your life through the principle of First Fruits

Cover and interior design by Roark Creative, www.roarkcreative.com.

ISBN 978-1-616580869-4 (hardback)
ISBN 978-1-61658-870-0 (paperback)

TABLE OF CONTENTS

DEDICATION

I pray the revelation God has given me on the principle of First Fruits will transform your life as it has mine and countless others! I gratefully dedicate this book to the Lord Jesus Christ...who became 'the firstfruits:'

But every man in his own order: Christ the firstfruits; afterward they that are Christ's at his coming. (1 Corinthians 15:23)

This book is also dedicated to all of our Covenant partners and friends of Paula White Ministries around the globe, who have grasped this divine principle of First Fruits and seen the fruit of it at work in their lives. To all of our Covenant partners and friends I say "thank you" -- for helping me transform lives...heal hearts...and win souls throughout the world. May God richly bless you for your faithfulness!

FOREWORD

You may know my history—how God reached down to a Mississippi girl who was devastated by the suicide of her father as a child . . . who was sexually, physically and emotionally abused . . . who felt worthless and used up . . . and who was full of mistrust and hurt in her life. He reached down with His loving arms and cradled my broken heart in His own hands. He accepted me with all my imperfections, just as He does you. But that was only the beginning! He had a divine plan.

From the moment I heard the gospel for the first time and dedicated my life to God, I knew I had a heavenly Father who loved me and who had a purpose for my life. Now, I certainly didn't know exactly what that purpose was or how I was going to accomplish it, but I knew the answer was found in God's Word. I held up the Bible and declared, "The answers to life are in here—reveal to me who You are, and who I am. Reveal to me 'life answers.'"

For two years, with a passionate hunger and insatiable thirst for the Word of God, I studied day and night. During that process, God imparted a vision in my spirit. In that vision there were masses of people as far as I could see. Every time I opened my mouth, there was a manifestation of the presence of God. When I shut my mouth, people would fall off a cliff into darkness. With that, God clearly impressed in my spirit that He had called me to preach the gospel. He showed me that a day would come when every time I opened my mouth, nations would be changed. I knew God wanted to use me to preach to the far reaches of the earth. I was not about to give up on that vision—and He didn't either. But even though I knew the vision was from God, I also knew I had to wait to see it come to pass in His timing and in His way. Though I did not know how, I knew in my heart that He was going to amplify my voice one day for His purpose and glory.

This book is just one of the realizations of that promise. What an awesome privilege and pleasure to serve God. As I sought God's plan for my life, He gave me a greater hunger to really "excavate" the roots of His patterns and principles in order to teach the Body of Christ. The teaching of first fruits is one of those critical principles. I began to study everything I could about this principle. And when I began to get the revelation of this, I said, "God, your people need this word!"

I am passionate about seeing people released from bondage and lack to walking an empowered life in the fullness of what God has given—those precious and magnificent promises available through our true knowledge of Him. Knowledge comes from studying the Word. Then comes revelation, and that is what motivates us to move in faith! I have found that the "lack" in any area of our life is not because of a provision shortage, but most often because of a revelation shortage. Now, let me take you deeper in what was revealed by the Word of God to me. I believe it will change your life just as it has mine.

Paula

INTRODUCTION

Are you ready to "live the High Calling" life God meant for you to live? Are you ready to live an ultimate life with purpose, provision, blessings and fullness of His presence? There is a high calling . . . an ascended life in Christ that is a way of life available for you. To "ascend" is to "walk up" or "step up." As you step forward, you are going to step up! It doesn't matter where you are today or what your situation, the God I serve has an amazing life for you. Nothing is impossible with God!

He created the sun, moon and stars by speaking them into existence. It is almost beyond comprehension! Imagine serving the God who showed up as the fourth man in the fiery furnace with Shadrach, Meshach and Abednego and in the lion's den with Daniel's den. He parted the waters of the Red Sea to let His people cross upon dry ground. My God is the same God who showed up at a widow woman's house during a severe famine and caused her barrel of oil to never fail and her meal to never run out. He's the same God who controls all of eternity.

This is the God who wants you to experience peace, hope, health, provision, wholeness and purpose. In order to do so, He laid out His patterns and principles in His Word for us to follow and obey as we serve Him

I've heard that Smith Wigglesworth said, "Nothing is impossible with God. All the impossibility lies in us, when we measure God by the limitations of our own understanding." So any time there is less than "life more abundant," it means we are living beneath our covenant privileges—we're living short of God's desire and provision for our lives. There may be seasons of "lack," but there should not be a lifestyle of it. For the purpose of clarification and understanding, to be in "lack" means to be deficient or without in any area of your life. That includes your spirit, soul and body. God has a "whole" life for you. Jesus declares in John 10:10, *"I am come that they might have life, and that they might have it more abundantly."* The word "abundantly" means in the sense of beyond, superabundant in quantity or superior in quality. By implication, it means excessive! God has an "excessive life" for you. Are you ready to live it?

Part of what drives me to preach, to teach, and even to write books comes from experiencing it myself and seeing that many of God's people are not prospering in their spirit, soul and body! They are not living the fullness of what God sent His Son as a sacrifice to give to us— abundant life. I see lack either in love, or joy, or finances, or health, or peace of mind, or household and family. I talk to people all the time who love the Lord and serve God faithfully, but they struggle day-to-day, week-to-week, month-to-month—just to survive. I know what that is like; I have been there. I know many folks who live "paycheck to paycheck" fearing that at any moment something could happen that would completely wipe out their finances; people who love God but are emotionally depleted and dysfunctional, stressed out, sick, fearful and all too often defeated.

Why are God's people living with lack—that is,

tolerating fear and anxiety, sicknesses and disease, living with stress and torment, addictive behaviors and habits—instead of experiencing what God has declared and desired for them that is a life of "wholeness?" We clearly cannot blame God. He is the god of the impossible. Obviously the problem is not on His end. So what is it that we might be missing? His best plan for our life. What is holding us back from living and coming into alignment with the abundant life Jesus talked about? Why can't we move into the realm that God has already established over our lives? I believe it is not that we are doing everything "wrong" . . . sometimes we are just not doing enough of what is "right." When you "know better, you live better."

One of the most powerful principles of God's Word is that of first fruits. It is found in Matthew 6:33, *"But seek first the kingdom of God and His righteousness, and all these things shall be added to you" (NKJV).*

God says first things first! You will not experience the fullness of "abundant life" and promises of God without the foundation of first fruits. It is prioritizing His presence in your life. It's the order and accurate arrangement of things. The principle of first fruits provides the foundation and structure for God's blessings in your life.

There is a pattern laid out for your success, for your well-being and abundant life. There is a pattern laid out for your peace and protection. There is a pattern laid out for your family and future. There is a pattern laid out for your career and calling. It's already been fashioned and formed by the master architect. You just have to serve in obedience to God and follow His pattern.

I know personally the power of first fruits. At the beginning of every year, in the month of January, I invite all my ministry friends and partners to join me in dedicating ourselves to a holy time of consecration with prayer, fasting and the giving of a first fruits offering. January is the first month of our year, and the first establishes the rest. It is a principle that what is established as first will govern the rest. We want to start our year with the discipline of fasting and consecrating ourselves to God, to seeking His presence as priority for our lives that year. We also present our first fruits of the year to the Lord in the form of one day's salary, one week's salary, or even one whole month's salary as each person has the faith and ability to give. We are not simply "saying" He is Lord, we are "showing" He is Lord as instructed in His Word.

Since I began to understand and apply the power of the first fruits principle, I have seen provision in my life. Many of the significant things in my life happened out of first fruits or coming in obedience and alignment with the order of God. Believe me, when you act in faith, trusting God that the root governs the rest, you will discover the life God puts you into is bigger than the life you are living.

When we put God's will first in our lives, all else falls into place. In the following pages, I want to share this life-changing principle to help you release all the blessings and success God has for you. I pray that as you read and study, you will have eyes of understanding that open the realms of revelation. The Holy Spirit will show you the mysteries, or sacred secrets of God!

Chapter 1
First Things First

Wouldn't it be nice to know where you're going in life, have the abundant means to get there and enjoy the journey? I believe you can.

God has a perfect design and purpose for your life. And He wants you to have the ability and resources you need to accomplish that divine destiny. You may be thinking, "Wait a minute, if that is so then why is my life so chaotic? I never have enough energy, emotional stamina, associations or finances. I feel like I'm at my wit's end struggling to survive. And how do I even find God's plan for my life?"

A simple principle from God's Word holds your answer. It's found in Matthew 6:33, *"But seek first the kingdom of God and His righteousness, and all these things shall be added to you" (Matthew 6:33).* "Seek first" is a foundation principle that has changed my life. And it can transform yours, too! Keep first things first, and God will take care of the rest.

When you put God first by obeying His principles and following His divinely established patterns, your life becomes aligned with His plan and purpose. But all too often, we get thrown off-track by the worries and clutter of life. You see, when we step out of God's perfect plan, we get off-balance.

And when you are off-balance spiritually, it spills over into every area of your life. Nothing else seems to fit and you don't feel whole. Your emotions, relationships, finances and health can suffer. But wholeness is prospering in your spirit, soul, mind and body. While it includes your finances, prosperity is not materialism, it is a wholeness word that means everything prospering, everything functioning properly in your life.

What good is it to have money, and yet be bankrupt in your spirit? As Jesus said, *"For what shall it profit a man, if he shall gain the whole world, and lose his own soul?" (Mark 8:36).*

When you are whole and in alignment with God, you can experience peace, joy, restoration, love, a right mind, freedom and liberation. And you should have enough resources to do everything that God has assigned in your life and called you to do. Read the entire biblical context of "first things first" in Matthew 6.

> *"Therefore I say to you, do not worry about your life, what you will eat or what you will drink; nor about your body, what you will put on. Is not life more than food and the body more than clothing? Look at the birds of the air, for they neither sow nor reap nor gather into barns; yet your heavenly Father feeds them. Are you not of more value than they? Which of you by worrying can add one cubit to his stature? So why do you worry about clothing? Consider the lilies of the field, how they grow: they neither toil nor spin; and yet I say to you that even Solomon in all his glory was not arrayed like one of these. Now if God so clothes the grass of the field, which today is, and tomorrow is thrown*

> *into the oven, will He not much more clothe you, O you of little faith? Therefore do not worry, saying, 'What shall we eat?' or 'What shall we drink?' or 'What shall we wear' For after these things the Gentiles seek. For your heavenly Father knows that you need all these things. But seek first the kingdom of God and His righteousness, and all these things shall be added to you"* (Matthew 6:25-33).

That is "prosperity" and peace of mind. That is wholeness! And that is what I want to help you achieve by sharing the importance of keeping first things first.

GOD'S ORDER

The key is to align yourself with the patterns of God. His principles were established long before man ever had a revelation or a vision of them. They are unchanging. And as I've said before, God's principles propel you into His promises!

A pattern is an order of arrangement or parts . . . a model or a design from which copies can be made. For every pattern, there is a design and for every design there is a designer. It is not your job to design or to develop, but to discover and implement or put a decision and plan of God into effect. Patterns are established from concept, the original intention, thought or notion.

God's original intention is His final decision. That means God doesn't change his mind—His patterns are permanent. All that God creates is "perfect," including you! You were created with a God-intended position and purpose. That intention will not change. In other words, as a surrendered, yielded life, if something is not supposed to be a part of your destiny, it will not be. You cannot lose what is supposed to be part of your destiny and you cannot keep what is NOT a part of it.

God still considers first things to be holy and devoted to Him, but today first fruits has to do with the practice of keeping the Main Thing—the main thing, and God IS the main thing! First fruits means the first in place, order and rank; the beginning, chief or principle thing. God says first things belong to Him in order to establish redeeming covenant with everything that comes after. In God's pattern, whatever is first establishes the rest. The first is the root, from which the rest is determined.

What a release from pressure to try and make life happen, or force something to fit! Proverbs 19:21 reminds us that *"many are the plans in a man's heart, but it is the Lord's purpose that prevails."* Plans are the contrivance of a mentally fabricated plot. What a waste of time, energy and talent when God's ultimate intention will always succeed!

All you need to do is "flow" with the determination of God. You have been positioned, or "accurately arranged," to simply walk out the pattern or predetermined plan of your destiny! You do so by implementing His principles. When a divine principle is implemented, a divine result is reaped.

So what is God's original intention for you? From the very beginning, God states His purpose and carries it throughout His entire Word. He wants to conform His character in you individually . . . that you will look like Him, act like Him, think like Him, walk like Him, talk like Him and create like Him. As we individually embrace this continual process of change a transformed "people," or "church" will come forth to bring reformation and advance the kingdom of God. You will live in His image, complete and whole. That means you will be fruitful. You will grow and increase in the abundance and anointing of God. You will be replenished . . . you will take dominion and subdue.

How do you live out your destiny? Because God is a God of patterns, when you follow the pattern, you see the manifestation of the promise from being in position. All covenant privileges are released and received by believing and activating the Word of God. That's why you must have the truth of God's Word operating in your life for all things to comply and agree with the determination of God.

So if your life is spinning out of control, it is time to clear the clutter and put first things first according to God's patterns and principles.

I have often said, "You cannot conquer what you don't confront; you cannot confront what you don't identify." What is throwing you off? Fear? Unhealthy relationships? Finances? Improper motives? Your purpose or destiny? Your emotions? Poor health? Later in the book, I'll share how you can clear the clutter in these areas of your life by aligning your priorities with God.

God has an arrangement for things in your life. When something is arranged, it is put into a proper or systematic order. God has a time and a purpose for everything.

"To everything there is a season, A time for every purpose under heaven; A time to be born, And a time to die; A time to plant, And a time to pluck what is planted; A time to kill, And a time to heal; A time to break down, And a time to build up; A time to weep, And a time to laugh; A time to mourn, And a time to dance; A time to cast away stones, And a time to gather stones; A time to embrace, And a time to refrain from embracing; A time to gain, And a time to lose; A time to keep, And a time to throw away; A time to tear; and a time to sew; A time to keep silence, And a time to speak; A time to love, And a time to hate; A time of war, And a time of peace" (Ecclesiastes 3:6).

God has an order and a plan for you. To be in harmony with the will of God and attain the highest state of purpose for your life, you must follow God's precepts. If you fail to keep God first, your life can become out of balance and out of order.

Many precious believers have bypassed and overlooked the principle of first fruits in God's Word, perhaps not intentionally but unknowingly. If it's important to God, it must be important to us! This principle is foundational, even fundamental for the manifestation of God's promises and provision to come to pass in our lives. As I have experienced in my own walk with God, this principle unlocks many, many doors and releases promise for the purpose of God in the earth.

It is so simple, yet has the power to impact every area of your life—your well being, your spirit, your soul, your body, your marriage, your relationships, your finances—every single area. Through the truths of first fruits, you can position yourself in God's order of things.

I want to direct your attention to a key scripture having to do with first fruits. *"And thou say in thine heart, My power and the might of mine hand hath gotten me this wealth. But thou shalt remember the LORD thy God: for it is he that giveth thee power to get wealth, that he may establish his covenant which he sware unto thy fathers, as it is this day" (Deuteronomy 8:17-18, KJV).*

God is the only One who has the power to give wealth, which is a word of wholeness that is nothing missing and nothing broken, and blessings—that is a life of empowerment. But it is exciting to know that He has given us the knowledge we need to receive those blessings. His truths are available to you. His commands and blessings are outlined in God's Word for all who will search them out to see.

IGNORING THE TRUTH?

Sadly, too many people either ignore or fail to learn about the principles of God's Word. And the lack of

PROVISION OF OBEDIENCE

During the days of Elijah, there was a widow who lived in a town called Zarephath. A severe famine fell over the land because there had been no rain for crops or herds. They were in a deep recession. So naturally, that is where God sent His prophet.

> *"When [Elijah] came to the town gate, a widow was there gathering sticks. He called to her and asked, 'Would you bring me a little water in a jar so I may have a drink?' As she was going to get it, he called, 'And bring me, please, a piece of bread.'*
>
> *"'As surely as the LORD your God lives,' she replied, 'I don't have any bread—only a handful of flour in a jar and a little oil in a jug. I am gathering a few sticks to take home and make a meal for myself and my son, that we may eat it—and die.'*
>
> *"Elijah said to her, 'Don't be afraid. Go home and do as you have said. But first make a small cake of bread for me from what you have and bring it to me, and then make something for yourself and your son'" (1 Kings 17:10-13, NIV).*

Can you imagine? Elijah would seem rather audacious, but you have to understand … he was operating under revelation of first fruits with an understanding of the faithfulness of God and a love for people. He wanted the best for this woman and her son. The love God puts in you for those that He "assigns" you to often moves you to act on revelation with a boldness and authority. God had already told Him that He had commanded a widow in Zarephath to provide for him. That part is easy to understand. But what would make that poor widow—who had conceded that she and her young son were to suffer death by starvation over the coming days—give any of what she had to a stranger? Revelation, or the uncovering and discovering of God's truth.

Elijah told her not to be afraid because, *"The LORD, the God of Israel, says: 'The jar of flour will not be used up and the jug of oil will not run dry until the day the LORD gives rain on the land'" (1 Kings 17:14, NIV).* In the face of despair, that widow woman suddenly got revelation from the man of God. He told her to give her first fruits—even though she had next to nothing—to him, and she would receive the blessings of God. She was reminded to put God first and she willingly obeyed, bringing Elijah the water and cake he'd requested. As a result of her first fruits offering, *"there was food every day for Elijah and for the woman and her family. For the jar of flour was not used up and the jug of oil did not run dry, in keeping with the word of the LORD spoken by Elijah" (1 Kings 17:15-16, NIV).*

No matter what situation you may be in, you have the Word of the Lord just as this widow woman did and God will always honor your obedience to His Word!

knowledge of God's Word brings death to things that should be abundant in your life. It causes you to lean on the arm of the flesh and make decisions from that position more than trusting in God. Wherever there is lack in an area of our lives, we should search our hearts—and His Word—and find out what is missing, or perhaps what we don't know.

When Jesus was being tempted in the desert to turn

the stones into bread, He answered, *"It is written: 'Man does not live on bread alone, but on every word that comes from the mouth of God'" (Matthew 4:4, NIV)*. God's Word cannot fail to operate in our lives when applied appropriately. Yet with all the teaching, prophecy, books, tapes and different versions and colors of the Bible that are available today—people are still perishing for a lack of knowledge of God's Word, and not doing what God has revealed through His Word (see James 1:22). It takes application with understanding to see the provisions and promises of God flourish in your life. This does not mean we will obtain every fleeting desire and whimsical want in our life. It does not mean we will never have any challenges, obstacles or even disappointments on our journey. What it does mean is that the Word of God will guide, equip and transform you by His truth for the intention of God.

We must question if we are bored with the Truth. Are we so well fed on God's Word that we have become numb to its principles and precepts? We must heed the word of the prophets of long ago, and set our hearts to knowledge and understanding. We cannot approach the Word of God with a "cafeteria and buffet-style dining" attitude. In other words, we cannot pick and choose what we want or have a "taste" for at that moment. We must eat of the full discourse of His Word.

I personally know what it is to live in a place of "lack" for a long time—a lack of love, wholeness, provision, protection, security and peace. I also know what it is to live in "abundance," to be content in all things with a peace that passes all understanding and to have provision for each season and an inner fortitude to build the life God had masterfully designed for me.

If we will gain God's greatest blessings, we must embrace His highest purpose. I do not want you to have lack in any area of your life, and I am going to do everything I can to show you the things that God has revealed to me over the past several decades that will show you how to live in the fullness of His covenant.

The key is living according to God's patterns and principles. You cannot plead promise and violate principles to see provision from God. There are costs to attaining God's best. If we want to have His greatest provisions, we must be willing and obedient to live a yielded and surrendered life. We must be willing to give to God what we love the most. Just as there are results for being out of alignment with God, there are rewards for keeping His divine patterns. Following, or aligning yourself, with God's principles and policies brings positive results and a satisfied life.

✶Always remember: Abundance is not limited to financial increase. In His parable of the sheep and the good shepherd, Jesus is the one who gives life (as opposed to the thief who kills), and life more abundantly, meaning for sheep: good pasture, safety, health, guidance, etc. Just as lack is not limited to affecting only your finances, likewise, abundance relates to every area of your life. Many believers would ponder why, if "provider" is the nature of God, they would not see this manifestation in their life. Part of the answer is that the provisions of God are not given randomly or to support selfishness or the fulfillment of "fleshly" desires and demands. Much like Abraham—who had been brought to a place of spiritual fulfillment when he had to choose between his love for God and his love for what God had given him when the Lord commanded him to take Isaac, his son, to Mount Moriah—we will come to a crossroad in decision of surrendering our greatest loves and desires to God! The provisions of God are without limit to those who give their "all" to Him!

NO SECRET TO GOD'S BLESSINGS

God has good things for you—He *wants* you to be blessed. That is why He tells you exactly how to go about receiving His abundance.

> *All these blessings will come upon you and accompany you if you obey the LORD your God:*
>
> *You will be blessed in the city and blessed in the country. The fruit of your womb will be blessed, and the crops of your land and the young of your livestock—the calves of your herds and the lambs of your flocks. Your basket and your kneading trough will be blessed. You will be blessed when you come in and blessed when you go out.*
>
> *The LORD will grant that the enemies who rise up against you will be defeated before you. They will come at you from one direction but flee from you in seven.*

The LORD will send a blessing on your barns and on everything you put your hand to. The LORD your God will bless you in the land he is giving you.

The LORD will establish you as his holy people, as he promised you on oath, if you keep the commands of the LORD your God and walk in his ways. Then all the peoples on earth will see that you are called by the name of the LORD, and they will fear you. The LORD will grant you abundant prosperity—in the fruit of your womb, the young of your livestock and the crops of your ground—in the land he swore to your forefathers to give you.

The LORD will open the heavens, the storehouse of his bounty, to send rain on your land in season and to bless all the work of your hands. You will lend to many nations but will borrow from none (Deuteronomy 28:2-13, NIV).

What an exciting list of blessings and provision! This passage gives us a glimpse of the depth and purpose of God's blessings. The word "blessed" really means to be *empowered to prosper and to succeed*. When you are empowered, you live life with an advantage.

Essentially every aspect of life is included in the blessing of Deuteronomy 28. Moses gave great detail in this passage to explain the blessings available to the children of Israel before they even took their first steps into the land of promise. These blessings were critical to their success in claiming the land God had provided.

It is the same with you and me. Ultimately, we only glorify God when we, like Jesus, accomplish the work that He has given us to do (John 17:4). Everywhere you go, your children, your herds, your flocks, your crops, your barns (in modern terminology that means your business, your bank accounts, your relationships, your mind and your home) will all be blessed and overflowing with the presence of God and His goodness, and everything you put your hand to will prosper. And your success glorifies God!

We will take a closer look at the depth and width of God's covenant of provision—His blessings, His fullness, anointing, abundance, restoration and more—throughout this book. But understanding the principles and order established by God in His Word is the key to living under this umbrella of divine confirmation, endorsement and supernatural results.

So if you feel out of balance or off-track today, there is hope. You can experience God's blessings! Within the pages of this book, I'm going to outline the process by which you can keep first things first and release all the benefits of His goodness. If you are living without focus, I want to show you from God's Word how you can begin to see a perfect alignment of your unique destiny with God's plan and purpose. Learn how to clear the clutter in your life and keep first things first through the principle of first fruits.

Chapter 2
You can have a BIG LIFE!

God has a plan. That plan is always working. And that plan includes you! God has a BIG LIFE for you. He has designed a life of wholeness, one that is blessed and successful, for you to enjoy—one that has peace and purpose, joy, goodness, completeness, wealth, health and fullness.

I consider John 10:10 to be on of the main mission statements of Jesus' ministry on earth. He said, *"The thief cometh not, but for to steal, and to kill, and to destroy: I am come that they might have life, and that they might have it more abundantly."* The Amplified version of the Bible reads: *"...I came that they may have and enjoy life, and have it in abundance (to the full, till it overflows)."*

Imagine a Big God doing big things in you and through you without worry, fear, anxiety, pressure, stress and confusion. He has for you a life of vitality, energy, stamina, clarity, love, value, purpose, fulfillment, provision and supply. He wants an intimate relationship with you and to establish His image in your heart and life.

God has supply for you. Proverbs 3:9-10 tells us as we honor the Lord with our substance and with the first fruits of all our increase, then there will be a filling to overflow and our presses will burst with new wine. "New wine" refers to expulsion, something squeezed out. In other words, what has been occupying that space will be driven out so that it may be filled with the blessings and provision of God for your life.

Peter proclaimed that God has given us *"everything we need for life and godliness through our knowledge of him who called us by his own glory and goodness" (2 Peter*

1:3, NIV). God is not limited by any problem ... He is not limited by a government ... and He is certainly not limited by the enemy. He is God. Everything you need has already been provided! As Paul said in Ephesians 3:20, *"Now unto him that is able to do exceeding abundantly above all that we ask or think, according to the power that worketh in us, unto him be glory in the church by Christ Jesus throughout all ages, world without end."*

The word and promises of God are for your everyday living. God intended for us, His children, to practice His habits and apply His laws. In the first chapter, I shared the amazing provisions of Deuteronomy 28. These promises cover your work, your relationships, your financial security, your victory over enemies, your future and so much more. They are without compare! And that is only beginning to "scratch the surface" of the in-depth, vast results and rewards for putting things in proper order—"first things first." All throughout the Word of God we see what happens when there is activation and honoring of first fruits. For example:

- Blessings will rest on your house. *". . . to cause a blessing to rest on your house" (Ezekiel 44:30, NKJV).*

- An angel will go before you to prepare the way, to tackle your adversaries for you. *"Behold, I send an Angel before you to keep you in the way and to bring you into the place which I have prepared" (Exodus 23:20, NKJV).*

- You will receive multiplication of provision for more than enough to meet your needs completely (John 6:5-13).

- You will have the power to get wealth. *"And you shall remember the LORD your God, for it is He who gives you power to get wealth, that He may establish His covenant which He swore to your fathers, as it is this day"* (Deuteronomy 8:18, NKJV).

- You will experience good health. *"Behold, I pray that you may prosper in all things and be in health, just as your soul prospers"* (3 John 2, NKJV).

BLESSED WITH WHOLENESS

These passages of Scripture are not just talking about God's power to meet your physical needs. God wants to take you further than that—He wants you whole, spirit, soul and body. As I said before, prosperity is a wholeness word. Though it includes financial provision, in Deuteronomy 28 and throughout the Word, we see that it means so much more. God's prosperity is really about everything in your life functioning and operating correctly. It is about divine completion. God wants you to have a balanced life. He wants your business affairs, your family, your emotions, your ministry and every part of your life to prosper to the same degree "as your soul prospers." If your soul is depleted, other areas of your life will be in lack as well.

The Bible declares in Psalm 115:14, *"The Lord shall increase you more and more, you and your children."* No matter what you have been through in your life, God has much greater things in store for you. According to the Word of God, I expect increase to come into your life as you continue to seek Him and He takes you from glory, to glory, to glory.

Psalm 5:12 reads, *"For thou, Lord, wilt bless the righteous; with favor wilt thou compass him as with a shield."* God will hedge you in with favor. Do you know what favor is? Favor is the kingdom of God giving you "undeserved access." God's favor takes you places and puts you in positions you could possibly never go on your own. It will take an orphan girl by the name of Esther and make her a queen for "such a time as this." Favor will raise you up out of obscurity into notoriety. Favor will cause Boaz (a "dream man" for a husband) to find you, Ruth. Favor will pull you out of the pit and put you into a palace, Joseph. Favor will turn your famine into a feast. Favor will promote you. It will put you in association with the right people. It will give you access to places that have been closed off to you. It will do for you what your résumé cannot do for you—what money, a mate, or ministry cannot do for you but the grace of God can do.

I am not implying that there will never be difficult times or bad things that happen. Bad things do happen to good people. Challenges will arise and there may be days of disappointment and difficulties—life has ebbs and flows. It is part of the rhythm to life. Your "faith" does not prevent "life" from happening, but it will carry you through it! As a believer you have been equipped to face whatever setback, obstacle or challenge comes your way through God and His Word. What I am saying is, you can have the peace that passes all understanding even when things are rough. You can have wisdom to navigate your life. You can have a patience and longsuffering to stand firm under pressure. You can have joy that far surpasses a happiness derived from external factors. Anything that the enemy steals from you, there is restoration. Anything you willingly offer up to the Lord will always come back as a blessing. God has promises for you that cannot fail. So people may see you in a pit, but they will also see God cause you to be triumphant over your circumstances and promoted to a palace if you don't quit during the process! God wants to be magnified and show Himself big in your life that He may be glorified.

With that favor, God will also protect you as with a shield. Like Solomon wrote in Proverbs 10:22, *"The blessing of the Lord, it maketh rich, and he addeth no sorrow with it."* In the Amplified it reads, *"The blessing of the Lord—it makes [truly] rich, and He adds no sorrow with it [neither does toiling increase it]."* Not only will you be blessed, you will be protected. It is the Lord who gives you the ability to get wealth—the power to prosper and to succeed in your unique destiny.

It is part of His covenant. Taking pleasure in prospering His children has to do with fulfilling His promises. Again, God is most interested in conforming the character of Christ in you. You are then transformed into His image where you think like God, act like God, talk, walk and create like God! It's not so much that we've been doing what is wrong that nullifies the provision of God. We need to understand that we're often not doing enough of what is right. I want you to think about that a moment. Partial faith does not open up the promises of God, but fully committed acts of faith do.

THE COVENANT

Jehovah is a covenant-making and covenant-keeping God. The Bible is a book of covenant. In fact, both the Old and New Testaments could be called the Old and New Covenants. A covenant deals with transactions between God and man, or man and his fellow man. It is a legal, binding contract. It is God's law. It is God's order. It is God's ways. A divine covenant is a sovereign disposition of God where He establishes an unconditional or declarative compact with man. He obligates Himself, in grace, to bring to pass of Himself definite blessings for the covenanted ones. Or it is a proposal of God where He promises in a conditional or mutual contract with man to grant special blessings provided that man fulfills perfectly certain conditions. Jesus is the basis and foundation of every covenantal purpose. All of the covenants consummate in Him who is the Heir and sum of all things (Hebrews 1:2, 8:1). Jesus secured the promises made to the fathers—Abraham, Isaac and Jacob. He then shared His "wealth" with us, the Bride, or the Church! All born-again believers are the seed of Abraham (Galatians 3:29, 4:1-2) and have a rightful spiritual estate and inheritance. Jesus Christ was the fulfillment of the Davidic Covenant. Jesus is the One who established the New Covenant. He is the Head of the Church and as born-again believers we are His brethren who are conformed to His image (Romans 8:14-29, 2:6-13). The Abrahamic Covenant, the Davidic Covenant and the New Covenant are all interrelated; each one is an extension of the other all with promises and blessings now offered to us, His Church. They are legally and permanently ours in Christ. God cannot and will not deny Himself. He remains faithful to His covenantal Word. However, we cannot claim our promised inheritance until we know who we are in Christ. To know "who" we are in Christ is to know what we have in Christ. It is a covenant with terms and a promise that God will bless you with everything He is and everything He has.

As covenant people, we are joint heirs and co-laborers with Jesus Christ. He said, *"And I bestow upon you a kingdom, just as My Father bestowed one upon Me, that you may eat and drink at My table in My kingdom"* (Luke 22:29-30, NKJV).

But we cannot expect the multiple blessings of God to manifest in our lives if we are not holding up our end of the covenant. While God will always fulfill His part, are you fulfilling yours? There are specific requirements for all those who walk by faith. You have to do it God's way. Hosea 4:6 declares, *"My people perish because of lack of knowledge."* What we don't know can destroy us. You must have real knowledge and wisdom for the application of His patterns, principles and precepts to truly prosper.

What we learn from God's Word will sustain us, provide for us, care for our families and loved ones, give us victory, direct and protect our dream, set us free, bless us and so much more! *"Then Jesus said to those Jews who believed Him, 'If you abide in My word, you are My disciples indeed. And you shall know the truth, and the truth shall make you free'" (John 8:31,32, NKJV). "For the LORD giveth wisdom: out of his mouth cometh knowledge and understanding" (Proverbs 2:6).*

You must be careful to never minimize the majesty and the greatness of God. He is as big as you allow Him to be. I believe God's question to His people is, "Will you take the limitations off Me? Will you let Me be God? Will you not only learn my ways, but live according to my ways?" When you operate in His principles, you take off the limitations. The God who has prepared the blessing for you is the same God who is preparing you for the blessing!

According to Proverbs 2:6, knowledge comes from the study of God's Word. God gives wisdom, but out of His mouth—from studying and understanding His Word—we gain knowledge. We cannot fully comprehend the vastness of all God has for those who are His. But God has given us His Word to study and show us the mysteries or "sacred secrets" of God, in order to attain the knowledge we need to release God's plan and desire to prosper every area of our lives, as He confirms His covenant.

God's covenant is His law. With that covenant we have everything we need, every promise of God is ours when we apply and stand on His Word. As Peter wrote to those in exile after the resurrection of Jesus:

> *Grace and peace be multiplied to you in the knowledge of God and of Jesus our Lord; Seeing that His divine power has granted to us everything pertaining to life and godliness, through the true knowledge of Him who called us by His own glory and excellence. For by these He has granted to us His precious and magnificent promises, so that by them you may become partakers of the divine nature, having escaped the corruption that is in the world by lust (2 Peter 1:2-4, NASB).*

God guarantees you these wonderful promises by His Word. That's all He needs. God cannot break His Word. If He says it, it will happen—guaranteed! *"So shall My word be that goes forth from My mouth; It shall not return to Me void, But it shall accomplish what I please, And it shall prosper in the thing for which I sent it" (Isaiah 55:11, NKJV).* We can choose whether we will obey or disobey His commands. They are laid out to us for blessing . . . for an empowered and fulfilling life. They are laid out with consequences. If we choose not to obey the instructions God gives us, we face the consequences of those decisions. Isaiah 1:19 and 20 declares, *"If you be willing and obedient you will eat the good of the land . . . But if you resist and rebel, you will be devoured by the sword."*

We must have a fresh revelation of God's truth from His Word. We need to understand His covenant and His principles if we are going to walk in His fullness. We must see through the eyes of God with His perception. Without seeing from the perspective of God we can become frustrated, and wasteful of time, energy and talents.

When reading the magnificent list of blessings in Deuteronomy 28 and throughout God's Word, we cannot overlook the principle or condition connected to those blessings: "If you keep the commands of the Lord your God and walk in His ways..." There are principles throughout God's Word, and these principles are key to your receiving and walking in the promise of His covenant blessings. In other words, as we are obedient to walk in His ways…we will walk in His promises and provision.

How it must break God's heart to see His children doing without when He has given us everything we need. God wants to take you from increase to increase (Psalm 115:14). He has good things for you! God's promises are exceedingly great! Imagine yourself in a position of wholeness, perfect peace, redeemed, restored and promoted.

But you can't reach high ground holding onto lower levels. A BIG GOD doesn't live in "little places." He doesn't "inhabit" a place of bitterness, unforgiveness, jealousy, envy, rebellion and the "like." God does His part and you must do your part. That's the covenant. But what is "our part"?

IN AGREEMENT WITH GOD

According to Hebrews 11:6, *"But without faith it is impossible to please him: for he that cometh to God must believe that he is, and that he is a rewarder of them that diligently seek him."* Now, it is important to understand "please Him." It has nothing to do with getting God to like us or approve of us. He already loves you more than you can imagine. And that love is unconditional.

The Greek word for "please" means to come into alignment or to come into agreement with God. In other words, without the Word working in your life, it is impossible for you to come into alignment or think like God, see like God, act like God, create like God, and do like God. You cannot separate God from His Word. He makes Himself synonymous or "One" with the Word. John 1:1 says, *"In the beginning was the Word, and the Word was with God, and the Word was God" (NIV).* So without faith, it's impossible for me to line up or agree with the Word.

"So then faith comes by hearing, and hearing by the word of God" (Romans 10:17, NKJV). So, if you have faith, or the activated Word of God, you can see God's promises revealed. All you need is a Word, one revelation. You can take that revelation and work the Word and watch the Word work in and for you.

Faith is the Word and the Word is faith. That is why the Bible says God's people perish for lack of knowledge... lack of knowledge of the Word...lack of having the Word deep in their spirits...lack of acting on that Word. When we are not in alignment with God, when our minds are not renewed by His Word, there is lack, loss and even death to areas of our life.

I want to see the prophetic promises, the promises of revelatory ministry, of the Word of God manifested in your life. I want to position you for abundant life! I want you to experience the fullness of His presence. Isn't it time to stop living with lack, with death, and start living as God desires? God is no respecter of persons. He does not want to bless one person and leave someone else behind. He wants everybody individually and corporately to manifest the promise that He has for them.

There are so many promises and provisions God has planned for you. He wants to give you freedom, redemption, restoration, authority and abundance. He has a divine plan for your life that is full of victory. But to receive the promises, you must understand His principles from His Word.

That is why I want to do everything I can to help you get the principle of first fruits deep into your spirit. It is a fundamental law of God. And the laws of God are always working for you or against you. The choice is yours. Throughout this book, I want to help you dig deep into the Word and discover God's plan and priorities to help you build an intimate relationship with Him, to fulfill your unique destiny and to see His abundant blessings released into your life. Hebrews 12:1 instructs us to *"lay aside every weight, and the sin which so easily ensnares us."* Let's start there.

Chapter 3
Clear the Clutter

Genesis 3:9 (NIV) says, "But the Lord God called to the man, 'Where are you?'" It's a significant question to ask yourself. To simply "exist" would be a waste of your life. In order to live a life of purpose, you must do an examination. You must take inventory and audit your life authentically. When you are living outside your destiny, the plan and purpose God has for you, there will be an underlying frustration that is felt. If you are not living the abundant life of purpose Jesus Christ came to give you it's not that God isn't doing His part. Everything you need has already been given! So the question you must ask yourself is . . . why is it not working for me? What adjustments need to be made?

Too many Christians fail to live according to the law of first as outlined in Matthew 6:33 and all throughout the Word. It is often because of the problems and influences of "life" that crowd out their spirit. They fail to focus on what matters because of excesses, entanglements and chains to the past. I know, I have been there before.

We all have that closet in the back of the house . . . our junk closet. There are valuable items in the closet to be sure. But those items are hard to find amidst all the worthless junk. It's the same with our lives. When we are packed with clutter, we rob ourselves of value.

Clutter diminishes clarity.

Clutter robs valuable time

Clutter drains energy and creativity.

Clutter impedes movement or progress.

Clutter detracts from efficiency and effectiveness.

So what's the junk cluttering up your life? It is

anything that crowds your life from building, edifying and enriching your spirit. Spiritual clutter is made of emotions, mindsets, habits and past history that you harbor and hold in your soul and self, which makes you unable to nurture and support your purpose in life. How do you clear the clutter? Remember that the BIG LIFE God has for you *will* arrive when you surrender your small for God's BIG!

LESSONS FROM ABRAHAM

I want to help you dispel the confusion and chaos and discover some of the possibilities why you are not living to the fullness of your potential. Remember, you can't conquer what you don't confront. And you can't confront what you don't identify. Look at Abraham's life.

Just like Abraham, the father of our faith, we are covenant people—God's chosen for kingdom rule, realm and royalty. But, like many, Abraham had a problem. Let me set the scene. God had not yet changed his name to Abraham, but had given him a promise of blessings.

"Now the LORD had said to Abram: 'Get out of your country, From your family and from your father's house, To a land that I will show you. I will make you a great nation; I will bless you And make your name great: And you shall be a blessing'" (Genesis 12:1-2, NKJV).

Scripture goes on to say, *"So Abram departed as the LORD had spoken to him, and Lot went with him" (Genesis 12:4, NKJV).* There was the problem—Lot. The Bible doesn't say Abram asked or invited Lot to go. It just said Lot went. You see, Lot was a leech. He probably saw that Abram was going somewhere and latched on . . . tagged along. We'll always have people in our lives like that . . . who suck the life right out of us. But it wasn't so much a Lot problem ... it was an Abram problem.

We're often not so direct in our disobedience that we rebel against God. But we have weak natures that are not strong enough to say "no" to what's holding us back. We don't always know how to establish healthy boundaries.

There may be people or habits in your life that are just hanging on and pulling you back from your God-given destination. Your Lot is a distraction. A distraction is an "inappropriate attraction." You are not solely responsible for another's wellbeing. You can't make them happy . . . you can't make them OK . . . and you can't heal them. Only God can do that.

And if you continually hold others up in life, you will not only cause trouble for yourself, but you will take away their empowerment and make them a victim to you! Let God be God. We must learn to let go of things and or people that are not to be attached to us. Separate yourself from the Lot in your life.

Separation brings revelation and revelation produces worship. Worship always brings exaltation. This is a continuing cycle of separation—revelation—exaltation. God takes us through levels, which include a form of separation, and with each one we get closer to our promise. This famous progenitor of our faith made seven critical decisions of separation, each one bringing him to a "higher" place in his life and walk with God.

If you are stuck and struggling to receive the fullness of what God has for you, then perhaps there is something in your life that needs separation. I encourage you to get up and get out from what is holding you back from all that God has for you. Following the seventh and final separation, God revealed Himself to Abraham as Jehovah-Jireh, the God who sees and provides, which means complete, unlimited provision without any further requirements. Only then, could he experience that abundance. He had to be separated from country and culture (Genesis 12:1), kindred (Genesis 12:1), Egypt (Genesis 13:1), Lot (Genesis 13:1), a desire to get wealth (Genesis 14:21-24), Ishmael (Genesis 17:18/21:9-14) and Isaac (Genesis 22:1-4). His son Isaac was who he loved most, what he had waited for. This was the ultimate test and worship in its purest sense.

ARE YOU OFF-BALANCE?

It took Abraham 25 years from the time God makes the promise before he sees anything take place. Why? When Abraham starts off on his journey, he got sidetracked and settles in Haran, the city with the same name as his brother who had died. Abraham settled in a place of his past. He was stuck between a past pain and a promise for the future. It took a crisis, his father's death, to get him moving again on his divine course.

When Abraham does move on, Lot goes with him. Lot is the son of Abraham's dead brother. Probably out of guilt or shame, Abraham feels responsible for Lot. He is living an imbalanced life. He was probably driven to rescue and fix Lot, which was not his responsibility. When you are out of balance with God's precepts, anything can become an external solution to calm the internal chaos.

Consider these eight common excesses that are symptoms of an imbalanced life:

- Eating too much. Overeating, binge eating and mindless eating are often symptoms of a greater issue in your life.

- Chemical pleasures. People use drinking, smoking and drugs to fill a void or cover pain.

- Overworking. If you are pre-occupied with your career to the detriment of your relationships, it becomes an excess. Is your career or job your whole identity?

- Overspending. Excessive pursuit of materialism, hoarding and clutter reveals a personal problem.

- Rescuing people. If you find yourself continually drawn to people who need a savior, you might want to re-examine your own motives. Do you expect too little out of others?

- Putting up walls. If you distance yourself emotionally from others, there is a reason. Do you expect too much out of others? Are you afraid of being hurt?

- Overthinking. With obsessive thinking and

analyzing, you may be avoiding your feelings.

- People pleasing. If you are an excessive people pleaser, you are letting a fear of rejection rule your life. You can't please everyone.

Behaviors like those above are driven to excess from dysfunction. Maybe you have a relationship in your life that has become an entanglement, a snare and a complication. Is there a Lot in your life? An unhealthy Lot relationship can be characterized by controlling behavior, distrust, perfectionism and intimacy problems.

Lot represents:

- Ungodly attachments—any person, mindset, habit or attitude you hold against God's Word, such as unforgiveness, bitterness and malice. Let it go!

- Disobedience—to God's Word and calling over your life.

- Distraction—such as inappropriate attraction.

As long as Lot is in your life, you are stuck. But if you will clear the clutter and let go of people and things that are not part of your covenant relationship and responsibility, God will help you move above your situation and see with a clearer and more accurate healthy perspective.

THE PAIN OF DISOBEDIENCE

Joshua 7 gives an account of when the children of Israel disobeyed God and transgressed their covenant. After the victory of Jericho, God had commanded a ban for His people on the spoils of the city. *"But all the silver and gold, and vessels of bronze and iron, are consecrated to the LORD; they shall come into the treasury of the LORD" (Joshua 6:19, NKJV).* The first spoils of warfare belonged to God! All firsts belong to God!

"But the children of Israel committed a trespass regarding the accursed things, for Achan . . . took of the accursed things; so the anger of the LORD burned against the children of Israel" (Joshua 7:1, NKJV). "Accursed thing" in the Hebrew is *charam.* It means dedicated or devoted to religious uses.

As a result, they suffered defeat in the battle against the men of Ai. When Joshua pleaded before God as to why they were defeated, the Lord replied, *"Get up! Why do you lie thus on your face? Israel has sinned, and they have also transgressed My covenant which I commanded them. For they have even taken some of the accursed things, and have both stolen and deceived; and they have also put it among their own stuff" (Joshua 7:10-11, NKJV).*

God does not "curse you," but your direct disobedience brings consequences that can hurt you and others, and potentially be tragic. When you knowingly and directly walk out of the covering of God's protection and provision for your life, you are "vulnerable" to threats, attacks and harm. Achan took what belonged to God—a first or devoted thing—and put it with his own stuff. Because of disobedience, the children of Israel could not stand before their enemies. That is why God declares, *"To obey is better than sacrifice" (1 Samuel 15:22).*

REASONS FOR LACK

If you've tried to clear the clutter in your life before but found yourself back in the same situation over and over again, there may be other deeper issues in your life that need rooting out. There are several reasons the Bible gives for having lack in our lives. I want to encourage you to examine your life and take practical action to root out what is hindering you from achieving all that God has for you. Here are some deeper issues, unwanted characteristics and bad habits that may be standing in your way. Your life will be sabotaged until you can "locate" and discover what it is that obstructs your fullest potential.

An unteachable spirit. Proverbs 13:18 says, *"Poverty and shame shall be to him that refuseth instruction: but he that regardeth reproof shall be honoured."* The New Living Translation puts it this way: "If you ignore criticism, you will end in poverty and disgrace; if you accept criticism, you will be honored." There have been many times I was so grieved and felt deep concern or sorrow for someone who suddenly decided they needed no accountability or teaching. When you stop learning, you stop growing. Anyone who will lead must know what it is to be led.

We should all be teachable, no matter who we are, no matter what our social status may be, no matter what God has called or appointed any of us to do in our lifetime. We must continually maintain a teachable spirit, ever learning, ever humble before God. *"Humble yourselves in the sight of the Lord, and He shall lift you up" (James 4:10).*

You could study just one scripture all your life and never get the fullness of the revelation of it. There is so much more depth to God and His Word than we have even begun to understand. A philosopher once wisely stated, "I am the wisest man of all for I have come to understand that I know nothing."

Remember what God told the Israelites: *"Today, if you hear his voice, do not harden your hearts as you did at Meribah, as you did that day at Massah in the desert..." (Psalm 95:7-10).* God was angry with them for 40 years and they never entered His rest—His best—for them because they were a "stubborn and stiff-necked people." They were unteachable. If you wonder if you have had an unteachable spirit, ask the Lord. Seek the Holy Spirit—He will show you.

Laziness. God's Word tells us that we become new creatures the moment we accept Jesus as our Savior. That does not mean we instantly experience a new environment, new circumstances, new situations or new relationships. We become prosperous, successful and healthy when we receive God's Word, speak God's Word, meditate on it day and night, and live by it (Joshua 1:8). It takes effort to speak, effort to read and effort to study and meditate on God's Word, and effort to do that every day, day in and day out.

The Bible warns against laziness, *"Yet a little sleep, a little slumber, a little folding of the hands to sleep: So shall thy poverty come as one that travaileth; and thy want as an armed man" (Proverbs 24:33-34).* Anyone who thinks God is going to simply rain His blessings down on you while you sit back and take it easy—you've been deceived. Laziness will never allow you to experience the fullness of the promises of God. Ecclesiastes 5:3 states, *"For a dream cometh through the multitude of business; and a fool's voice is known by multitude of words."*

We must live by faith, but we are also to put works with our faith (see James 1:22). We are to act, to move out in that faith. You have to be a doer of the Word, not just a hearer.

Ignorance. *"My people are destroyed for lack of knowledge" (Hosea 4:6).* It doesn't get much clearer than that. And notice who is destroyed: My people. People who love God and have a relationship with Him are destroyed because of ignorance, a lack of knowledge, an awareness of information. They are lacking in an abundance of life because of the things they do not know. As Solomon said, *"By knowledge shall the chambers be filled with all precious and pleasant riches" (Proverbs 24:4).* Perhaps you have heard the saying, "It's what you don't know that is killing you." I have found that you can have a "right heart" and a "wrong head," in which case you will live defeated or deficient in areas. As a child of God, it is vital to have a renewed mind (Romans 12:12) that possesses the perspective of God.

Oppressing the poor. Proverbs 22:16, 22 says, *"He that oppresseth the poor to increase his riches, and he that giveth to the rich, shall surely come to want … Rob not the poor, because he is poor: neither oppress the afflicted in the gate."* Oppressing another person means keeping them down. God warned the Israelites about the poor, saying,

"Give generously to [the poor] and do so without a grudging heart; then because of this the LORD your God will bless you in all your work and in everything you put your hand to. There will always be poor people in the land. Therefore I command you to be openhanded toward your brothers and toward the poor and needy in your land" (Deuteronomy 15:10-11, NIV).

God increases the person who takes care of the poor—the person who is openhanded instead of closed-fisted. It is something He is very serious about, even telling the Israelites not to glean every single grain from their fields or grape from their vines, in order to leave some for the poor to harvest for themselves. The Bible tells us that we are not aware that some strangers may even be angels. What if there was an opportunity for you to receive "promotion" by someone who was placed in your life who had a need that could be met by you, who was poor, and you ignored the urging of the Holy Spirit and bypassed that person? God will lead you in your giving to find someone that is in a less fortunate situation than you. Give to them. Giving is not isolated to dollars and cents. It may be food, a hug, education, love or time. Everything in life can be a "seed" to be sown into the life of another person. Altruism is one of the greatest blessings you can experience.

Misfortune. Sometimes lack simply comes from misfortune. This is clearly demonstrated in the life of the widow of Zarephath. Her story is found in 1 Kings 17. There was great famine in the land, and she had gone through nearly all of her flour and oil, having only enough left to make a small cake for herself and her son. After that, she anticipated starvation to set in, just as it had for so many others. Bad things can happen to good people. But God sent this little widow an opportunity. She had the option to take that cake for herself, and her son, or to make it for the prophet of God instead. That is a tough place to be. We all want to believe we would easily yield to a difficult decision because we are "so spiritual." The truth is, obedience can be difficult when you are in a "pressure situation." But she obeyed the illogical instruction of the prophet and God blessed her with abundance. The flour and oil did not run out throughout the entire famine and her household was not only preserved but prospered.

The Gospel is the book of Good News, and Romans 8:28 is exactly that: *"And we know that all things work together for good to them that love God, to them who are the called according to his purpose."* So when life does contain misfortune, look at it like this: "It's not my stumbling block. This is just a temporary thing. It's going to be my stepping stone. God's taking what was meant for bad and turning it around for good." Somehow, some way, there is "good" coming out of misfortune! Don't waste your trial but allow the painful places in your life to have purpose.

Disobedience. Deuteronomy 28 is all about the blessings of obedience and the curses of disobedience. I listed the blessings in the first chapter (Deuteronomy 28:2-13). But the curses are just as real:

> *If you do not obey the LORD your God and do not carefully follow all his commands and decrees I am giving you*

today, all these curses will come upon you and overtake you:

You will be cursed in the city and cursed in the country.

Your basket and your kneading trough will be cursed.

The fruit of your womb will be cursed, and the crops of your land, and the calves of your herds and the lambs of your flocks.

You will be cursed when you come in and cursed when you go out.

The LORD will send on you curses, confusion and rebuke in everything you put your hand to, until you are destroyed and come to sudden ruin because of the evil you have done in forsaking him... *(Deuteronomy 28:15-20, NIV).*

Part of getting "first things first" is to identify those things in your life that may be holding you back from walking in God's best. Once you can identify the problem, you are empowered to change it. If there is lack in your life, I encourage you to use the "spotlight" of God's Holy Spirit to identify—and conquer—whatever is holding you back. He will gently reveal to you erroneous areas and equip you for correction and direction.

Chapter 4
The First Fruits Principle

The Hebrew word for "first fruits," *reshiyth*, means the first in place, time, order or rank. It also means the beginning, first or principle thing, captain or chief, excellent, forefront, principal, ruler, sum, top, summit, upper part and primary. First fruits, which belong to God, govern the rest and set the pattern, or the promise, to come. Another Hebrew word for "first fruits," *bikkurim*, means "a promise to come." It shares the same root word *bekhor*, as the word meaning firstborn. The first fruits offerings signal the beginning of your harvest. It promises an abundant harvest. It establishes the law of first things first in your life. It establishes the promise of that which is to come and positions the believer to receive the promises of God.

Yom HaBikkurim, the Jewish festival celebrating the Feast of First Fruits, is one of the most mentioned feasts in the Bible, second only to Passover. God's Festivals or Holy Days reveals His cycle of worship and plan for the harvest of blessings and eternal life through the agricultural practices of the day. He declared His Holy Days as the people harvested their crops around three festival seasons. Three times a year God commanded His people to celebrate agricultural harvest festivals—the Festivals of Passover, Pentecost and Tabernacles. The Holy Days have meanings that build upon each other that illustrate God's patterns and principles. Passover is the barley harvest. Pentecost is the wheat harvest. Both are first fruits harvests before the final harvest at the end of the year during the Festival of Tabernacles, which is the fruit harvest. First fruits are the first part of the harvest to ripen.

It is the part of the harvest that was given to the priest as an offering to the Lord. The instructions on how each family was to bring a basket of their first fruits and give it to the priest as the Lord's representative (Deuteronomy 26:1-12 and Leviticus 23:10-14) gives specific guidelines for a special first fruits sheaf to the Lord at the time of the Passover festival. They could not begin their harvest of barley and other crops until the high priest had offered the first fruits sheaf to the Lord in a special ceremony. As the Lord of the harvest, God had to receive his special portion before the rest of the harvest could be reaped. It is also found in Ezekiel 44:30, declaring that except the priest receive the first fruits, a blessing cannot rest in the giver's house. We will examine this in greater detail further in this chapter.

God designed seven feasts (Leviticus 23). These feasts were God's own holy days with specific instructions given for their observance. The Hebrew word "feasts" means the appointed times. The sequence and masterful orchestration of these feasts or divine appointments demonstrates how all that follows in the Old Testament pointed to the cross and beyond. They illuminate supernatural truths and blessings for you today. God is a covenant keeping God. And, yes, we live under the New Testament that has provided through Jesus a better covenant with promise. While we are no longer held to the rigid set of rituals and routine, God still "holds us" to the principles for all these feasts to follow.

The day following the high Sabbath during Passover is called the Feast of First Fruits (Leviticus 23:10-14). It

SPIRITUAL BONUSES

In addition to the many blessings, first fruits accomplishes two other goals:

Proves Your Faith—*"Trust in the LORD with all thine heart; and lean not unto thine own understanding. In all thy ways acknowledge him, and he shall direct thy paths. Be not wise in thine own eyes; fear the LORD, and depart from evil. It shall be health to thy navel, and marrow to thy bones. Honour the LORD with thy substance, and with the firstfruits of all thine increase"* (Proverbs 3:5-9).

Brings Honor to God—*"LORD, I have loved the habitation of thy house, and the place where thine honour dwelleth"* (Psalm 26:8). By trusting in God with first fruits, you bring honor to God and give Him glory and respect.

celebrates and recognizes God's hand of blessing and provision over His people. The first fruits offering is seen as early as the times of Cain and Abel and is the only feast mentioned nearly as many times as Passover in the Bible. First fruits, or the principle of first things, has to do with a giving of the whole of the first, not just a part, as with the tithe. You may ask, "What is first fruits today?" The Jews had two new years—a civil and a religious. The principle behind the date is our focal point. There are designated starting points for the new years and the first fruits of the new year belong to the Lord of the Harvest. First fruits is the first or beginning of all things. When you start a new job, the first paycheck is first fruits and therefore it belongs to the Lord. When you get a raise on the job, an amount that reflects the increase on the first check is the first fruits.

The first day of the week is the Lord's. The first moments of the day belong to God. God is a god of divine order. First fruits is the first in place, order and the principle or essential thing. First simply means first.

In ancient days, the process of gathering the first fruits of the crops involved painstaking preparations. Each family among the Israelites had to carefully watch for the first budding fruits or grains. Once spotted, they would designate it as the first by tying a piece of red yarn around the branch, limb or vine.

As the crops matured and were harvested, those first fruits were brought into the Temple and presented to the High Priest according to God's pattern. The Priest would accept the offering from each household. *"The priest shall take the basket from your hands and set it down in front of the altar of the LORD your God" (Deuteronomy 26:4, NIV).*

Once they handed the priest the first fruits offering they were to proclaim the story of Isaac's journey into Egypt, how his descendants became a great nation, and the resulting slavery and their suffering. Then they verbally acknowledged how…

> *"…The LORD brought us out of Egypt with a mighty hand and an outstretched arm, with great terror and with miraculous signs and wonders. He brought us to this place and gave us this land, a land flowing with milk and honey; and now I bring the firstfruits of the soil that you, O LORD, have given me" (Deuteronomy 26:8-10, NIV).*

Finally, they were instructed to: *"Place the basket before the LORD your God and bow down before him. And you and the Levites and the aliens among you shall rejoice in all the good things the LORD your God has given to you and your household"* (Deuteronomy 26:10-11, NIV).

Other offerings of the first sheaves of wheat were for the land, but the first fruits offering described here related to the Feast. I can imagine the people marking their crops, waiting for those first fruits to mature and ripen—and how they must have naturally desired a taste of that year's very first grapes, figs, wheat, barley, pomegranates, olives, and dates. But they would put God first, taking their baskets out, separating each different fruit within the basket with some leaves, and presenting the best of the best unto the Lord.

But what happened to all those baskets of fruit afterwards? They were not consumed by fire. God didn't come down and eat them. So who did? The priests did. As God told Aaron, *"All the land's firstfruits that they bring to the LORD will be yours. Everyone in your household who is ceremonially clean may eat it"* (Numbers 18:13, NIV). Like other offerings, the first fruits offerings were part of what was used to support and feed those who ministered God's Word to the people. I'm going to give you a lot of scripture in this chapter because I want you to see this pattern. When explaining the appointed feasts to Moses, God said:

> *Speak to the Israelites and say to them:*
> *"When you enter the land I am going to*

*give you and you reap its harvest, bring
to the priest a sheaf of the first grain you
harvest. He is to wave the sheaf before
the LORD so it will be accepted on your
behalf; the priest is to wave it on the day
after the Sabbath. ... This is to be a lasting
ordinance for the generations to come,
wherever you live.*

*From the day after the Sabbath, the
day you brought the sheaf of the wave
offering, count off seven full weeks. Count
off fifty days up to the day after the seventh
Sabbath, and then present an offering of
new grain to the LORD. From wherever
you live, bring two loaves made of two-
tenths of an ephah of fine flour, baked with
yeast, as a wave offering of firstfruits to the
LORD... Then sacrifice one male goat for
a sin offering and two lambs, each a year
old, for a fellowship offering. The priest is
to wave the two lambs before the LORD as
a wave offering, together with the bread of
the firstfruits. They are a sacred offering
to the LORD for the priest...This is to be
a lasting ordinance for the generations to
come, wherever you live" (Leviticus 23:10-
21, NIV).*

Bringing the first fruits offering to the priests was a
lasting ordinance for the generations. Notice what God

says of the Levites:

> *"After you have purified the Levites and presented them as a wave offering, they are to come to do their work at the Tent of Meeting. They are the Israelites who are to be given wholly to me. I have taken them as my own in place of the firstborn, the first male offspring from every Israelite woman. Every firstborn male in Israel, whether man or animal, is mine. When I struck down all the firstborn in Egypt, I set them apart for myself. And I have taken the Levites in place of all the firstborn sons in Israel. Of all the Israelites, I have given the Levites as gifts to Aaron and his sons to do the work at the Tent of Meeting on behalf of the Israelites and to make atonement for them so that no plague will strike the Israelites when they go near the sanctuary"* (Numbers 8:15-19, NIV).

The Levites serving in such manner actually helped prevent plagues from striking the Israelites. God is the designer who established the pattern for us to follow. He never commanded us to understand Him but simply obey Him! As I stated before, God is not trying to hold anything back from you...He is trying to get things to you. Anything that is a first, a first thing, a first fruit, a first born, a devoted thing, God always lays claim to it. It belongs to God—not a portion of it—but the whole thing. God sees the first thing as the root that governs all the rest.

WHY THE PRIESTS?

God's Word is full of patterns, and the manner in which the first fruits were to be presented to the Lord was no different. In the Old Testament, the offerings were given to the priests and Levites so that they could be devoted to the work of the Lord and carry out His instructions for the people. But what was significant in the Old Testament about bringing the first fruits offering to the priests in such a manner? How did that benefit the one who brought the offering?

The key is found in the words of God to Ezekiel, *"And the first of all the firstfruits of all things, and every oblation of all, of every sort of your oblations, shall be the priest's: ye shall also give unto the priest the first of your dough, that he may cause the blessing to rest in thine house"* (Ezekiel 44:30, KJV).

Under the Old Covenant, the priest received the first fruits offering and waved it before the Lord as a means of presenting it to God. He then prayed to release the blessings of the Lord over the house of the one who presented the offering.

But let's take this apart a little. It says that the priest would cause the blessing to rest on your house. The first tendency is to think of the physical building in which you dwell. But the Israelites were living in tents at the time. The Hebrew term for "house" or "household" in this verse is "bayith," meaning family. It comes from the root word "banah," which means to "build." The blessing would rest not on your dwelling, but on your family…on your lineage…your children, grandchildren, their kids and grandkids and so on.

Joshua put a choice before the Israelites to choose who they would serve, the Lord or other gods. Then he gave his choice: "As for me and my house, we will serve the Lord" (Joshua 24:15, NKJV). Again, we tend to think "and my house" may include the husband, wife, and kids living there at the time. But actually it means generation after generation. The blessing comes to the house of the giver by a spoken word from the mouth of the priest. The Hebrew word for blessing is *berakah*, which means "benediction" and by implication "prosperity." It did not just come and go, but it came and rested. The Hebrew word for rest is *nuwach*, which means to settle down, to dwell, to stay or fall in place. It is the very heartbeat of a loving God to grant you a "household blessing!"

Not all denominations have a "priesthood" any longer, nor do the priests and leaders live off the fruits and slaughtered animals of the sacrifice. The equivalent today would be bringing your first fruits offering to the man or woman of God with whom you are in covenant and or partnership with. The man or woman of God is blessed and encouraged by your giving first fruits. 2 Chronicles 31:4-5 declares, *"Moreover he commanded the people that dwelled in Jerusalem to give the portion of the priests and the Levites, that they might be encouraged in the law of the LORD."*

This is vitally important! We live in the most

powerful prophetic time in the destiny of nations with the manifested presence of God in our midst. God is releasing His heavenly pattern for advancing His kingdom. Breakthrough believers are being raised up to impact and influence our world in ways never seen before. God's purposes cannot and will not miscarry. He is being perfected in a people to complete His purpose in their spirits . . . to bring forth His plan and purpose in the earth. He is reproducing the very life of Jesus Christ in the "fragile earthen vessels of human clay." It is "Christ in you," the hope of glory, rising up unto maturity and being formed within you (Galatians 4:19).

How will this come to pass? *"And he gave some, apostles, and some, prophets, and some, evangelists, and some, pastors and teachers; for the perfecting of the saints, for the work of the ministry, for the edifying of the body of Christ; Till we all come in (unto) the unity of the faith, and of the knowledge of the Son – of – God unto a perfect man, unto the measure of the stature of the fullness of Christ"* (Ephesians 4:11-13). It is the five-fold ministry gifts that God chose as His divine instrument to bring the "saints into perfection." The word perfection means complete furnishing, to complete thoroughly, i.e. to repair or adjust. In essence, if the five-fold ministry gifts can be shut down, then the "mature church" or Bride of Christ can be shut down! No wonder Ezra 6:13-16 declared that the children of God continued to build and prosper under the preaching of the prophet and the priest.

DEVOTED TO THE LORD

The principal of first fruits was not limited to vegetation. It is found throughout the Word, and deals with all "first things." *"Do not hold back offerings from your granaries or your vats. You must give me the firstborn of your sons. Do the same with your cattle and your sheep" (Exodus 22:29-30, NIV).*

Throughout God's Word, He tells us that *every* devoted thing, or first fruit, is most holy unto the Lord. Notice the instructions God gave to Moses as He prepared the Israelites to be led out of slavery in Egypt:

> *"And it shall be when the LORD shall bring thee into the land of the Canaanites, as he sware unto thee and to thy fathers, and shall give it thee, That thou shalt set apart unto the LORD all that openeth the matrix, and every firstling that cometh of a beast which thou hast; the males shall be the LORD's. And every firstling of an ass thou shalt redeem with a lamb; and if thou wilt not redeem it, then thou shalt break his neck: and all the firstborn of man among thy children shalt thou redeem" (Exodus 13:11-13).*

God claims the right to every first—the first of the crops, every firstborn male of herds and flocks, every first-born male child. Every first is to be devoted to God through His covenant. Any time something is called a first

THE ULTIMATE SACRIFICE

Jesus is the fulfillment of the Old Covenant practice of sacrificing the first and best to God for redemption.

1 Corinthians 15:23 says, *"But every man in his own order: Christ the firstfruits; afterward they that are Christ's at his coming."* Romans 8:29 says, *"For whom he did foreknow, he also did predestinate to be conformed to the image of his Son, that he might be the firstborn among many brethren."*

God gave His first and only Son as the sacrifice for our sins. Jesus was the manifestation of first fruits. He was the first-born of Mary (Matthew 1:23-25, the first-begotten of God the Father (Hebrews 1:6), the beginning of the creation of God (Revelation 3:14), the firstborn of many brethren (Romans 8:29), and the first fruits of the resurrected ones (1 Corinthians 15:20, 23). Jesus is the choicest and the first.

Since Jesus was crucified on the day of Passover, the fourteenth of Nisan, and He arose from the grave three days and nights after He was crucified, Jesus arose from the grave on the seventeenth of Nissan—the day of the Festival of First Fruits. He is the first fruits of the family of God!

thing, a first fruit, a devoted thing, it belongs to God. And, if it is devoted to Him, the Word of God declares that it is better to destroy it than to use it for yourself.

In Exodus 22:29, God instructs Israel again saying, *"Thou shalt not delay to offer the first of thy ripe fruits, and of thy liquors: the firstborn of thy sons shalt thou give unto me."* The Amplified reads, *"You shall not delay to bring to Me from the fullness [of your harvested grain] and the outflow [of your grape juice and olive oil]; give Me the firstborn of your sons [or redeem them]."*

The principle is that <u>all</u> first things belong to God.

Even in the midst of rebuilding their destroyed city, Nehemiah restored and kept to this pattern, and Jerusalem was protected as a result:

> "...and that they might bring the first fruits of our ground and the first fruits of all the fruit of every tree to the house of the LORD annually, and bring to the house of our God the firstborn of our sons and of our cattle, and the firstborn of our herds and our flocks as it is written in the law, for the priests who are ministering in the house of our God. We will also bring the first of our dough, our contributions, the fruit of every tree, the new wine and the oil to the priests at the chambers of the house of our God..." (Nehemiah 10:35-37, NASB).

In Leviticus 27:28-29, God again explained the instructions for first fruits: "But nothing that a man owns and devotes to the Lord—whether man or animal or family or land—may be sold or redeemed; everything so devoted is most holy to the Lord" (NIV). Devoted things and first things have the exact same meaning, which is "the irrevocable giving over to the Lord." In other words, they are the things that belong to God and to God alone. All first things belong to God. If you touch these devoted things, you remove yourself from the covering God has for you. On the other hand, when you obey the principle of first fruits, you'll see the strong hand of God favor, protect and provide for you.

God sees the first thing as the root governing all the rest. *"For if the firstfruit is holy, the lump is also holy; and if the root is holy, so are the branches"* (Romans 11:16, *NKJV*). When the first governs the total, whatever the first portion is used for determines what happens to all the rest. If a first thing is consecrated to the Lord as "holy" then it sanctifies the rest as "holy" or having the presence, endorsement and blessing of God on it.

FIRST THINGS

God has established certain firsts all throughout His Word:

First Commandment— *"And Jesus answered him, 'The first of all the commandments is, Hear, O Israel; The Lord our God is one Lord: And thou shalt love the Lord thy God with all thy heart, and with all thy soul, and with all thy mind, and with all thy strength: this is the first commandment'"* (Mark 12:29-30).

First Time of the Year—*"And the LORD spake unto Moses and Aaron in the land of Egypt, saying, This month shall be unto you the beginning of months; it shall be the first month of the year to you. Speak ye unto all the congregation of Israel, saying, In the tenth day of this month they shall take to them every man a lamb, according to*

the house of their fathers, a lamb for an house"
(Exodus 12:1-3).

First Born—*"And the LORD spake unto Moses,*
saying, Sanctify unto me all the firstborn,
whatsoever openeth the womb among the children
of Israel, both of man and of beast: it is mine"
(Exodus 13:1-2).

First Fruits—*"The first of the firstfruits of thy land*
shalt thou bring into the house of the LORD thy
God" (Exodus 23:19).

First Dough—*"Ye shall offer up a cake of the first*
of your dough for an heave offering; as ye do the
heave offering of the threshingfloor, so shall ye
heave it. Of the first of your dough ye shall give
unto the LORD . . ." (Numbers 15:20-21).

First Spoil—*"Out of the spoils won in battles did*
they dedicate to maintain the house of the LORD"
(1 Chronicles 26:27).

SEEK YE FIRST

God is very serious about things being in order in
our lives. That is why it is so crucial that we understand
this principle of first things first. When you do not put
first things first, there is disorder, which can affect your
life. On the other hand, when you do put first things first,
your life can and will fall into place as it is supposed to.

Just as God promised—when we are faithful to follow His commandments, we will live an empowered life and be blessed!

God is not a god of confusion (1 Corinthians 14:33). The Greek term for confusion means instability, inconstant and unstable and is often translated as disorder. Notice what James said, *"For where envying and strife is, there is confusion and every evil work" (James 3:16)*. Strife means a division, a faction, a pulling away. Where there is division there is confusion—disorder—which opens the door for every evil work and practice and then every evil spirit. The reason some of us are fighting such demonic spirits and influences is because we have had disorder—"to move away from the pattern"—in our lives. Often times we hit a "crossroad" in life that causes us to step back and re-examine. It is the place of authentic inspection that makes us mirror our life to the Word of God and ask . . . Where is the wholeness? Where is the provision? Where is that sense of everything working properly and in order? Remember, God is a god of order.

Remember, a "first" is a fundamental principle or a basis supporting existence or determining essential structure or function. It is the one thing that affects or governs everything that follows it. If the first is holy, the remainder will be holy.

A principle is a fundamental truth or a law upon which others are based. It is a rule of conduct. Principles always have policy. Policy comes from the word "police." Police is "a governing agency or department that provides order." So the way you govern your life or rules of conduct must be by the fundamental laws or truths of the Word of God in order to see the promises or rewards that God has for you. His Word is always working for you or against you!

THE PRINCIPLE REMAINS

Thankfully, we no longer sacrifice the firstlings of our sheep or cattle at a Temple; nor are we required to redeem our firstborn sons with gold. Jesus paid for all redemption through His death, burial and resurrection, giving us a New Covenant *"founded on better promises" (Hebrews 8:6, NIV)*. Jesus was God's first and only begotten son. He gave up His son to set Him apart as holy first fruit. The first fruit then sanctified all who came after so Jesus became the first fruit of many brethren (Romans 8:29, 1 Corinthians 15:23). We bear forth the same power and image of God because we are the fruit of His firstborn.

However, the principle of first things still remains. God does not change in His character or principals. He is the same yesterday, today and forevermore (see Hebrews 13:8). While we do not hold to the ritualistic and routines of the annual "feasts" or divine appointments of God, for it is impossible to keep "exactly" the feasts. We are to honor and obey the principles and patterns. Jesus taught in Matthew 5:17-19 that the Torah (or first five books of the Bible) retains validity until the earth passes away! The implication and idea was that Jesus came to fulfill and establish the proper meaning and to bring to full expression or give fullness and provide true meaning, as opposed to destroying, overthrowing or abolishing.

We have to understand God's never-changing principle that in order to possess the promises He has for each of us we must come into alignment with His divine order, governed solely by His Word.

God loves you so much that He wants to rescue you from everything that pulled you out of the position and divine alignment He has for you. God wanted to bring us to Him, but even He would not violate His principles. So He sacrificed His Son. You cannot violate principles and expect to have positive results. I cannot stress enough the importance of following the patterns and principles of God!

The law of first things is the giving over, as required of <u>all</u> <u>firsts</u>! They are an offering in faith and they prove the position in which the giver holds God and is held by God. In Exodus 33, God installed requirements in His "system" of Lordship to ensure their confession was more than mere words. He established ways for His children to prove that He is first! The requirements were the Ten Commandments, the structure of the ritual of sacrifice, the statues of the Tabernacle and what we now call . . . "The Law of First Things!

Chapter 5
Putting First Fruits Into Action

Now that you understand the importance of keeping first things first according to God's perfect order, how do you apply the principle of first fruits practically in your own life? As I began to study and dedicate more and more time to seeking God's heart on this principle, I asked, "Lord, why don't we see it? We're speaking but the mountains are not always moving." Have you ever felt that way? It is all right to be honest and authentic with God and ask questions.

What I felt was revealed to me was that people are speaking, but speaking alone is not the precedent God has set. It is not the pattern of God. You can't put a roof on a house before having the foundation firmly in place. So let's go back to the beginning. In Genesis chapter 1, we see where God created the heavens and the earth. But notice verse 2, *"And the earth was without form, and void; and darkness was upon the face of the deep. And the Spirit of God moved upon the face of the waters."*

Notice what it says: the Spirit of God moves in darkness. The Spirit of God moves in empty wastelands. The spirit of God moves when there is a void. Do you have an area in your life right now that is void, without form and dark? Is there an area that is not in alignment or matching up with what God has said in His Word?

Verses 3 and 4 go on to say, *"And God said, 'Let there be light,' and there was light. And God saw the light, that it was good..."* So if we are speaking—expecting to see results—without *moving*, then we cannot expect to see the fulfillment of promises. Simply put: You cannot claim the promises of God while violating the principles of God.

A great example is the life of Hannah, the mother of the prophet Samuel (1 Samuel 1). Hannah was the wife of Elkanah, and to her shame and bitter disappointment, she had not been able to conceive. She deeply desired a child, and her own limitations became her focus. Elkanah's other wife, who was seeing God's promise fulfilled with the gift of many children, frequently provoked and tormented Hannah, bringing her to tears. Perhaps it was even unintentional, but often someone's "success" pours salt on the wound of our "failures."

So one day Hannah "stood up" (v. 9), and went to the Temple to pray. There she poured out all the bitterness and hurt to the Lord through her tear-filled sobs. I believe it was during that pouring out of her heart that revelation hit her spirit. She vowed, *"If you will only look upon your servant's misery and remember me, and not forget your servant but give her a son, then I will give him to the LORD…" (v. 11).* The revelation that hit her spirit took her eyes off herself, and shifted her focus to the Lord. So she gets up, wipes away her tears, straightens her clothes and heads home to her husband. Notice that her situation had not changed, but revelation had motivated her spirit.

Instead of giving up and feeling sorry for herself, she went home to Elkanah, and the Bible says, *"in the course of time she conceived and gave birth to a son" (v. 20).* Hannah put God first, put works with her faith, and conceived her promise! Revelation causes motivation for us to move when there is nothing. That is why I say we do not have a provision problem—far from it. Our problem is a revelation problem. Every irritation can be an invitation for elevation and promotion. When your faith is challenged by created tension to push out the promise of God for your life, embrace and move in that moment! It is the working of His mighty power, or according to the energy of the power of His might that makes mountains move!

POSITIONED FOR POSSESSION

If you desire to live the abundant life that Jesus gave His life to give you, it is not only possible, but God's Word tells us how to attain it! You've been positioned for possession by the price Jesus paid and the grace God has given you. But part of that possession is taking hold or ownership of the promises of God. You can plead the promises all day long and pray until you are blue in the face. But until you learn to live out God's principles, your pleading will be in vain.

God wants you to know Him as a God of grace and power. But He also wants you to know Him as the all-sufficient God. He wants to be your defender, your protector, your provider, your redeemer and more.

You cannot prepare yourself in a day. You must prepare yourself every day…day after day…for the rest of your days. As Hebrews tells us, *"Remember your leaders, who spoke the word of God to you. Consider the outcome of their way of life and imitate their faith. Jesus Christ is the same yesterday and today and forever"* (Hebrews 13:7-8, NIV). Many have gone before us who have learned to have faith in God's principle of first fruits. I encourage you to step out into the knowledge you now have, and do the same. As David said:

> *Your promises have been thoroughly tested, and your servant loves them. Though I am lowly and despised, I do not forget your precepts. Your righteousness is everlasting and your law is true. Trouble and distress have come upon me, but your commands are my delight. Your statutes are forever right; give me understanding that I may live (Psalm 119:140-144, NIV).*

The understanding of all of God's principles, including first fruits is found in His Word. John 8:31-32 says: *"Then said Jesus to those Jews which believed on him, 'If ye continue in my word, then are ye my disciples indeed; And ye shall know the truth, and the truth shall make you free'."* When Jesus says to continue in His Word, He means to remain, to endure, to stand firm under pressure, to abide and dwell.

And if we look up "disciples" in the original text, it means a learner or a pupil. And of course "free" in the Greek means to liberate, deliver, make free. Reading this same passage in the Amplified brings even more clarity: *"So Jesus said to those Jews who had believed in Him, 'If you abide in My word [hold fast to My teachings and live in accordance with them], you are truly My disciples. And you will know the Truth, and the Truth will set you free.'"*

As believers, it is the truth that you know, the truth that you have revelation of that makes you free, liberated,

83

delivered. Knowledge comes from the study of God's Word. These verses make it clear why we are to get the Word in our hearts and minds and stand on the Word at all times. You don't walk with God according to what you feel. You walk by what you know. Eve knew she was forbidden to eat of the tree in the center of the garden, but the enemy's cunning convinced her to act on her feelings

Patterns are permanent. Principles are working for you or against you every day. It is the law of God!

instead of on her knowledge—and that didn't work out very well. As David said, *"My eyes anticipate the night watches and I am awake before the cry of the watchman, that I may meditate on Your word" (Psalm 119:148, AMP).*

It is the truth or Word that you know that will bring the unchangeable promises of God in your life. The Word is your covenant, your legal binding contract. All privileges are released through believing and receiving the Word . . . and by understanding and applying God's principles.

The Word will give you revelation. And revelation causes motivation. It is the change of position or passing to another place with a continuous motion. You are motivated to move and act by the revelation of truth. Acting in faith on that revelation is what releases the promises of God in your life and allows you to break the limitations and labels that have been put on you!

We live by faith, and walking out and operating out of that faith is our responsibility. For every single person born, there is a God-intended position and purpose. And every position that is in the purpose of God comes with divine principles and policies. So, when you are in position, you are advantageously placed and enabled to do. This is an empowered life when you see the activation of His promises by divine principle and policies.

We have to create and establish an atmosphere that is focused on God and based on the principles of His Word. The principle of first fruits is part of that active "walking out" our faith in operation to release the promises of God. The first sets the precedent for the rest. The harvest of anything can always be traced back to the seed. In other words, the "fruit" is simply a result of the "root!" Again, I stress the importance of ALL firsts, when "given" to God, then have His "presence" governing the rest! That is the first thoughts of your day, the first day of the week, the first month of the year, the first of all your increase, and so on . . . ALL firsts!

FIRST FRUITS VS. Tithe

Many have thought that the tithe, our giving of a tenth of our increase, is the same as first fruits. But the Bible references first fruits, firstlings, or devoted things 32 times, and mentions the tithe 32 times. However, Genesis chapter 4, is the first time that God talks about first fruits, or firstlings, with Cain and Abel. The first time we see the tithe mentioned is in Genesis 14:18-20, when Abraham tithed to Melchizedek. They are distinctly different, although the tithe is the first tenth of your income, not just any tenth!

In Deuteronomy 14:22-23, the people receive this instruction: *"Thou shalt truly tithe all the increase of thy seed, that the field bringeth forth year by year. And thou shalt eat before the LORD thy God, in the place which he shall choose to place his name there, the tithe of thy corn, of thy wine, and of thine oil, and the firstlings of thy herds and of thy flocks; that thou mayest learn to fear the LORD thy God always."*

Nehemiah 10:38-39 explains it further, *"And the priest the son of Aaron shall be with the Levites, when the Levites take tithes: and the Levites shall bring up the tithe of the tithes unto the house of our God, to the chambers, into the treasure house. For the children of Israel and the children of Levi shall bring the offering of the corn, of the new wine, and the oil, unto the chambers, where are the vessels of the sanctuary, and the priests that minister, and the porters, and the singers: and we will not forsake the house of our God."* From this passage, we learn that:

- The church is the redeeming agency in the earth.

- The tithe is processed through the church.

- The church is the storehouse of heaven.

- There is a price to pay for neglecting the house of God.

Let's take a look at some of the basic principles of tithing based on Scripture. First, we are commanded to bring all the tithes—the first tenth of the whole or "of any income," the complete and perfect tithe. *"Bring ye all the tithes into the storehouse, that there may be meat in mine house and prove me now herewith, saith the LORD of hosts, if I will not open you the windows of heaven, and pour you out a blessing, that there shall not be room enough to receive it"* (Malachi 3:10).

God invites us to prove our faith, to test out His promises, to examine, investigate or try Him, through the tithe. 1 Corinthians 16:1-2 lets us know that there is a set day, or an appropriate time to give our tithes. *"Now concerning the collection for the saints, as I have given order to the churches of Galatia, even so do ye. Upon the <u>first day</u> of the week let every one of you lay by him in store, as God hath prospered him, that there be no gatherings when I come."* Notice it is collected on the first day of the week.

The tithe is not to be forgotten or excused. The tithe was something instituted even before the law (see Genesis 14:19-20 and 28:22).

And don't forget the power of tithing! According to Malachi 3:10-12, there is a five-fold blessing of tithing:

- Opened windows—*". . . and prove me now herewith, saith the LORD of hosts, if I will not open you the windows of heaven (verse 10)."* Windows are the area of lurking. In other words things hidden or without visibility will be released. The primary purpose of a window is to allow visibility or vision. A tither has the right to see their destiny with clarity.

- Poured out blessings—*". . . and pour you out a blessing, that there shall not be room enough to receive it (verse 10)."* To pour out means to draw out to the point of being empty. Your tithe draws the blessing out of you. Notice the emphasis on the word "you!" That God wants to "open" you and "pour" you! <u>You are blessed to be a blessing!</u>

- Rebuke the devourer—*"And I will rebuke the devourer for your sakes, and he shall not destroy the fruits of your ground (verse 11)."* God will cripple the "seed eater" or anything that comes to consume what you produce.

- Your blessing will always come on time—*". . . neither shall your vine cast her fruit before the time in the field (verse 11)."* To cast means to miscarry, abort or rob your spoil. <u>There will be no more miscarriages of your blessing</u>.

- God will establish your reputation for being blessed—*"And all nations shall call you blessed; for ye shall be a delightsome land, saith the LORD of hosts" (verse 12).* A delightsome land is a valuable thing, to be pleasurable. What wonderful provisions from our covenant of tithing!

Tithing is redemptive! So what exactly is a tithe? It is 10 percent of all income and increase. However, it is <u>NOT</u> just any 10 percent . . . it is the first 10 percent

HANDS OFF! SERIOUSLY

When you take something that belongs to someone else there are serious consequences.

In 1 Samuel 15, God sent word to king Saul through the prophet Samuel that He intended to *"punish the Amalekites for what they did to Israel when they waylaid them as they came up from Egypt" (v. 2, NIV)*. Then the Lord instructed Saul saying, *"Now go, attack the Amalekites and totally destroy everything that belongs to them. Do not spare them; put to death men and women, children and infants, cattle and sheep, camels and donkeys" (v. 3)*. The Amalekites were eternal enemies of God.

Saul was obedient to the Lord in the fact that he attacked the Amalekites, and God gave him victory *"from Havilah to Shur, to the east of Egypt" (v. 7)*. However, though God told Saul to completely wipe out every Amalekite, even their cattle, sheep and other livestock, Saul chose to keep the king of the Amalekites alive as well as *"the best of the sheep and cattle, the fat calves and lambs—everything that was good. These they were unwilling to destroy completely" (v. 9)*. Partial obedience is disobedience.

Saul's unwillingness to obey deeply grieved the Lord. When Samuel confronted Saul with the word of the Lord about his disobedience, Samuel asked, "Why did you not obey the Lord? Why did you pounce on the plunder and do evil in the eyes of the Lord?"

Saul replied, *"The soldiers took sheep and cattle from the plunder, the best of what was devoted to God, in order to sacrifice them to the LORD your God at Gilgal" (v. 21)*.

Saul knew that all of the plunder was devoted to the Lord. Yet, he and his men spared the best of what God said to destroy—for their own use. This decision would prove not only to be devastating to Saul but for generations to come. It was an Amalekite that eventually came back and killed Saul. You are probably familiar with the next verse, *"But*

Samuel replied: 'Does the LORD delight in burnt offerings and sacrifices as much as in obeying the voice of the LORD? To obey is better than sacrifice, and to heed is better than the fat of rams'" (v. 22, NIV).

This example, though not specifically about a first fruits offering, does illustrate how very serious God is about things He calls devoted. The Amalekites were devoted to destruction, and for Israel to take anything that was so devoted and use it for their own use—even to make sacrifices unto the Lord—was completely unacceptable to God. Saul lost his kingdom and was tormented the rest of his days, and due to his disobedience, the Amalekites continued to be an issue for Israel. God is serious about what He claims "ownership" to.

Exodus 34:20 declares, *"Redeem the firstborn donkey with a lamb, but if you do not redeem it, break its neck" (NIV).* In other words, it is better to destroy something that is devoted to the Lord rather than keep it for your own use. Holy things belong to the Lord, and the Lord calls first fruits or first things holy.

of your income. A tithe is a first fruit when presented to God first that qualifies it as the tithe. Because it is redemptive, by giving God His portion first, you then redeem the remaining 90 percent, which is yours to do as you please. The "first" thing determines how everything else will go. Therefore when you present your tithe to God it determines where His presence and glory is going and where you are putting your faith. Whatever you "pay" or "give to" first governs and covers the rest.

Notice in Proverbs 3:10, tithing and first fruits are mentioned as two different things: *"Honor the Lord with thy first fruits and all thine increase."* First fruits is the whole of the first. The tithe refers to the first tenth of the increase. It comes after first fruits. Remember, God has a divine accurate order and arrangement of things.

First fruits is not the same as the tithe. First fruits is the whole of the first and keeping first things first; of recognizing, remembering God as the one who gives you the ability to get wealth. First fruits relates to dedicated, devoted, "first" things. Devoted things and dedicated things have the exact same meaning: the irrevocable giving over to the Lord. Deuteronomy 26 gives a distinct delineation between the two offerings.

THE RIGHT KIND OF SACRIFICE

Giving God your first includes your time, your talent, your heart and the fruits of your labor. Consider that all firsts belong to the Lord: the first part of the day, the first day of the week (Sabbath), the first month of the year, and the first of our harvest—be it the wages for the first hour, the first day, the first week or month.

God tells us to *"Remember the sabbath day, to keep it holy" (Exodus 20:8, NASB).* We also find the term *zakar* used here for "remember" the Sabbath. The Sabbath is the first of your week. It is what sets the tone for how the rest of your week will go. We are to "first fruit" the Sabbath, to mark it as devoted to the Lord, for Him, not for our own use. We all lead busy lives, but the Sabbath is to be set apart as holy. Its primary purpose is not a day for shopping or working, nor is it a day for doing your own thing. It is a day for acknowledging and celebrating the

Lord, meditating on His Word, and rest.

Remember, understanding, knowledge and wisdom comes from studying the Word and establishes us (Proverbs 24:4-5). We have been given a designated day for worshipping, celebrating and obeying God and His Word in His house, "the church." We need to ask ourselves…what are we doing with it? Are we making it paramount according to the plan and pattern of God? Do we not forsake the assembling of ourselves together as commanded in Hebrew 10:25?

Similarly, what you do first thing in the morning sets the course for the rest of the day. When you wake up say, "Good morning Holy Spirit, I bless you and praise you today, and devote this day to you." Get your day started after you have worshipped and heard from the Lord. God knows you have need of many things, many tasks and things to do. Again, when you keep Him first, as Jesus declared, *"But seek first His kingdom and His righteousness…all these things will be added to you" (Matthew 6:33, NASB).* He did not say, "seek the kingdom of God." He said "seek ye *first* the kingdom of God." Putting God first is the fundamental rule of the kingdom prescribed by the Founder. But sometimes, putting God first can be a battle—a battle between the flesh and the spirit.

THE BATTLE BETWEEN FLESH AND SPIRIT

True biblical prosperity has been a grossly misunderstood and misused word. It has to do with much more than just your finances. The Hebrew word for prosperous is "shalom," which means safe, well, happy, friendly, welfare—i.e. health, prosperity and peace. It is the primitive root; to be safe (in mind, body or estate), figuratively, to be completed or to make complete. It is a "wholeness" word. It is a transformation of your heart and soul. Your life is transformed as your mind is renewed or "renovated." To renovate means to take away the old and put in the new.

> "Do not conform any longer to the pattern of this world, but be transformed by the renewing of your mind. Then you will be able to test and approve what God's will is—his good, pleasing and perfect will. For by the grace given me I say to every one of you: Do not think of yourself more highly than you ought, but rather think of yourself with sober judgment, in accordance with the measure of faith God has given you" (Romans 12:2-3, NIV).

I will refer to Deuteronomy 8, verses 17 and 18 frequently throughout this book because it is foundational to the principle of first fruits. It says, "And thou say in thine heart, My power and the might of mine hand hath gotten me this wealth. But thou shalt remember the Lord thy God: for it is he that giveth thee power to get wealth, that he may establish his covenant which he sware unto thy fathers, as it is this day." Paul certainly understood these words of God when he warned believers not to "think of *yourself more highly than you ought, but rather think of yourself with sober judgment" (Romans 12:3, NIV).*

The mind of the flesh says, "I've done all this with my abilities," but the mind of the Spirit acknowledges that He is the one who gives you the ability to get wealth. The Hebrew word "wealth" means a force, whether of men, means or other resources, an army, wealth, virtue, valor and strength. You see, we can look right over the term "remember" in Deuteronomy 8:18, because we all know that "to remember" means to recall, to be mindful of, to retain an idea or to commemorate someone or something. Often, the Hebrew word translated as "remember" does mean that. But in this and several other places, it means something more.

In this verse, the Hebrew word is *zakar*. "Thou shalt *zakar* the Lord your God…" *Zakar* means "properly remembered as a male of man or animal, as being the most noteworthy; to mark as to be recognized as male."

God commanded the Israelites to devote the first of their flocks and herds, and even their first-born sons to Him as a first fruits offering—to remember that it was God who led them out of captivity, that it is God that gives them the ability to get wealth. Now we see God using the word *zakar*, which means to properly mark as male…of Himself.

What did the process of marking the first-born male relate to? It relates to the principle of first fruits. Remember, the Hebrew root for first fruits is *bikkurim*, the same as the root for firstborn. So, we could read that scripture in a more literal translation to say, "But thou

94

shalt [first fruits] the LORD thy God: for it is he that giveth thee power to get wealth…"

It is not our ability to get wealth; it is God's. When we "remember" Him properly, by placing Him as the first and foremost through the application of the first fruits principle, we are prioritizing His presence in our life. Matthew 6:33 (NKJV) declares, *"But seek first the kingdom of God and His righteousness, and all these things shall be added to you."* When something is first, it denotes foremost in importance or rank. No wonder C.S. Lewis said, "When first things are put first, second things are not suppressed, but increased." When we activate the principle of first fruits by the prescribed guide of conduct through the mandatory offering that God commands—in Exodus 23:15-16:

> *You shall keep the Feast of Unleavened Bread (you shall eat unleavened bread seven days, as I commanded you, at the time appointed in the month of Abib, for in it you came out of Egypt; none shall appear before me empty); and the Feast of Harvest, the firstfruits of your labors which you have sown in the field; and the Feast of Ingathering at the end of the year, when you have gathered in the fruit of your labors from the field.*

—we are acknowledging that it is God who gives us the ability to prosper and succeed in every area of our life.

In other words, when we "first fruit" the Lord, He gives us the ability to get "wealth" or a great force. In this way, the principle of first fruits operating in our lives is the key to walking in the fullness of the promises of God. When we do not violate the principles...then we can claim the promises and see their manifestation in our life.

Every position of purpose comes with divine principles and policies. When you live by principles and in position, then you have positive results. The first fruits principle gives you the power to get the wealth and always be mindful to the fact "that He may establish His covenant." The governing rule of conduct according to the truth of what God has to say in your life brings forth positive results. It is not something you have to "feel," but simply obey His Word and follow His pattern. When you do, you will see God's results and promises in your life. You will be victorious and a conqueror as God has declared. People who live a life with positive results have some type of principles that they live by. It is their rule of conduct and prescribed way of living.

IT IS NOT ABOUT YOU

We must recognize that it is not our limited abilities that release the promises of God. It is not solely our getting up and driving to work every day that provides the paycheck at the end of the week. No, it is God who blesses and favors us. It is God who gives us the ability, the power, the anointing to get wealth, prosper and succeed. It is His goodness and kindness to us!

Once again I want to remind you that wealth is not

limited to your income. Wealth has to do with your whole being, it means nothing missing, nothing broken, nothing out of order (first things first). It means having the blessings that God lists in Deuteronomy 28:2-13 made manifest in your life: peace on all sides, protection, provision, healing, restoration, redemption, guidance, wisdom and everything that you need in life and for your unique destiny. As the psalmist wrote in Psalm 66:12, *"We went through fire and water, but you brought us to a place of abundance."* It does not mean that you will not have adversity or opposition or that everything will go your way. However, it is an assurance that everything is working according or in harmony to the purpose and counsel of His will. I say if it's not "God sent" it is "God-used!"

Yes, God wants to bless you, and those abundant blessings are predicated by keeping Him first in your life! God established that we honor Him throughout all generations with the giving of a first fruits offering. He declared that it is a holy ordinance to be kept forever. And we see in Deuteronomy 28:9, as well as in Deuteronomy 8:18, it is through His blessings that He establishes His covenant, causing others to see that the Lord is God! It not only proves your faith, but brings honor to God as well. *"Trust in the Lord with all your heart, And lean not on your own understanding; In all your ways acknowledge Him, And He shall direct your paths" (Proverbs 3:5-6, NKJV).* To honor means to promote or to give glory, or make glorious.

If you are walking according to the natural or carnal

man, you are not walking by faith; *"For they that are after the flesh do mind the things of the flesh; but they that are after the Spirit the things of the Spirit" (Romans 8:5).* Without faith, it is impossible to please or come in agreement and alignment with God. Further, a carnal, fleshly mind brings death according to Romans 8:7. The carnal mind is enmity against God. The word "enmity" means hostile, hateful, in opposition and adversary. I don't know about you, but these are very sobering words!

Let's break it down even further. I would say, based on these verses of scripture, as believers we can examine things that are dying in our lives and often trace them back to a decision made with a carnal mind. Again, it may not be a direct disobedience or rebellion that is causing you to make poor quality decisions, but learned behavior, bad habits or even lack of knowledge. It is time to be pro-active by taking ownership and responsibility for a renewed mind that comes in alignment with the thoughts of God.

On the contrary, everything that has life, peace and abundance, you can trace back to a decision made with a spiritual mind. Look at the fruit of your life. What do you see? Are your thoughts in alignment with God's Word? Are your relationships in alignment with God's Word? Are your emotions and soul in alignment with God's Word? Is your physical body in alignment with God's Word? Is your life and financial responsibility in alignment with God's Word? If you are to prosper as your soul prospers, you must examine what condition your soul—that is your mind, will and emotions—is in. It's the attitude of the heart that manifests itself on the outside.

From my own life experiences, I could take you through almost every emotional, psychological, physical, or natural disaster a person could walk through. For many years "death" and or destructive behavior was produced in my life from carnal mindedness. When I was just 5 years old, my father, my hero, committed suicide. Not understanding the reasons for his actions, my young mind embraced a faulty belief and decided somehow I wasn't good enough or that would not have happened. Our fragile family soon experienced financial and emotional devastation after the death of my father. A year later, a cycle of sexual abuse began to twist my life into even deeper places of confusion and shame. These events created a false belief system that impaired my perception of my true identity and authentic self. From that faulty belief system I behaved in self-destructive manners throughout my childhood and teenage years. I wish I could tell you all my ill-behaviors immediately ceased when I surrendered my life to Christ and began an intimate journey with God. However, it is a lifelong process of daily dependence on Him. His mercies and grace are new every day. He takes us from glory to glory with a continual growth and renewal each and every day we choose to press into His presence.

The starting point of my personal transformation was when I surrendered, accepting Christ as my Savior, and was born again, that my carnal mind that I'd grown so used to serving began a process of change. My mind began to be renewed on the Word of God. Even when I fell ill in the mid-90s and the doctors examining me said my lungs were only operating at a fraction of the normal percentage, the mind of the Spirit was my comfort. They gave me a bleak prognosis with not much hope, but I believed the Word of God for my healing. Abiding in the Word of God, doing things God's way, not only transformed my mind, but also gave me revelation to walk in the provision of healing that God had already made for my life. It was a gradual process of walking day by day in wisdom and faith. So it has been with every area of my life. His Word is my compass to navigate my journey. I have discovered that we must do our "part" and be responsible to build a healthy life and lifestyle with the "tools" we have to work with. However, we must build on the foundation of God and His "part." This is not a "magic formula" for quick fixes in life. It is an intimate relationship of trust, nurturing and companionship that is bound by a beautiful covenant given to us with unconditional love and acceptance. Some seasons you will simply walk out a "sovereign strategy" that your mind struggles to comprehend, but your spirit can trust!

The battle between the spirit and flesh permeates every area of our lives. *"For we do not wrestle against flesh and blood, but against principalities, against powers, against the rulers of the darkness of this age, against spiritual hosts of wickedness in the heavenly places" (Ephesians 6:12, NKJV).* Your problem is not always your boss . . . or your neighbor . . . or your spouse . . . or your pastor. Your problem can be the enemy of your soul who is battling to gain control of your life and your mind in order to rob you of all that God wants to give you. Matthew 18:7 says, *"For offenses must come . . ." (NKJV).* You will be challenged and tried, but you cannot fight a spiritual battle in the natural. You must deal with your problems in the realm of the spirit, through God's Word.

God has already released you from bondage. But the enemy rejoices when he sees that 2,000 years ago there was liberty provided through the blood of Jesus, and yet so many still stand on the outside of freedom because they don't understand or know how to properly exercise their authority and covenant rights.

God's provision for you is a complete package. Paul said, *"Set your minds on things above, not on earthly things. For you died, and your life is now hidden with Christ in God" (Colossians 3:2-3, NIV).* The decisions you make today will determine the quality of life you live tomorrow. Therefore make sure you have the thoughts and mind of Christ directing your daily life!

By keeping first things first, you bring your life into the order God has established. The first fruits set the pattern or establish the destiny of what is left. What is offered as a first fruits offering establishes the protecting hand of God on what follows. Don't wait until life throws you a "curve" ball. Walk out the patterns of God every single day of your life. When you do, you will build a firm foundation that will not be shaken. The "things" are added to you when the foundation is in place to be built upon. Psalm 11:3 (NKJV) reminds us, *"If the foundations are destroyed, What can the righteous do?"*

When you stand before the Lord and offer Him a first fruits offering —whether it is a full day's wage, a week's wage or a month's wage (that is the whole of the first), it is just one step, but it is certainly the "right" step to set in motion many wonderful manifestations and results in your life. You must work out your faith—believe day after day that God has seen your offering of first fruits and blessed the rest. Now live in the blessing for generations to come! God has given you the "blue print"—the pattern to follow in order to release what He has provided for you: abundant life!

Chapter 6
The Unacceptable Offering

In 26 years of studying God's Word almost daily, I realize I have only scratched the surface to even begin to fathom the richness, depth and vastness of His wonderful truth. But when something really puzzles me, I find that I just can't let it go until I dig deeper and get a better understanding of it. That is the "meditation" of His Word! To continue to chew on it until you can digest it and receive its valuable nutrition.

The difference between Cain's offering and Abel's offering had been such a mystery to me for a long time. When I initially studied the Word of God, I could not figure out what it was about Cain's offering that was unacceptable to the Lord. And why did Cain become so angry? As I began to gain more insight into the deeper truths and specifically the principle of first fruits, it all started making more sense and had more clarity.

It is possible that Cain and Abel were twins. We definitely know they were brothers, born to Adam and Eve. I think it is interesting to notice what Eve said after Cain was delivered: *"I have gotten a manchild with the help of the LORD" (Genesis 4:1, NASB).* Eve had been promised a son, one whose heel would crush the serpent's head. If you think about it, I'm sure she was still disgusted with that serpent! It is possible she thought Cain was the fulfillment of that promise, but it seems she really only gave partial thanks to God for the birth of her first-born son. That makes me wonder if Cain didn't already have issues from the day he took his first breath.

When the boys grew older, Cain began to work the ground, plowing, planting, and collecting a harvest from the various crops and trees. Abel began breeding and raising a herd of sheep, since man was apparently no longer on the vegetable-only Genesis diet that was enjoyed in the Garden of Eden before the Fall.

Commentators generally agree that God must have given some form of worship and oblation instructions to that very first family. Though no specifics are given in that regard, I believe God had established a pattern with Adam and Eve, explaining the nature of offerings to be made unto the Lord, and that pattern has continued throughout the generations. It is also clear that Adam, Eve, and even their children were able to hear the voice of the Lord and worship Him. Notice what happens after the first recorded offering:

> *"And in process of time it came to pass, that Cain brought of the fruit of the ground an offering unto the LORD. And Abel, he also brought of the firstlings of his flock and of the fat thereof. And the LORD had respect unto Abel and to his offering: But unto Cain and to his offering he had not respect. And Cain was very wroth, and his countenance fell" (Genesis 4:3-5).*

ABEL'S OFFERING

Most scholars agree that it would seem that the phrase, "in process of time," relates to the end or beginning of something. It literally translates, "at the end of days." This means when something has ended and now there is a first or beginning. Whether it was the beginning of a week, month or year is unclear. When the family came to worship God most scholars note that Cain brought an offering of fine flour, oil and frankincense. That is a gratitude offering. Abel also brought a gratitude offering and the firstborn of his flocks (or a first fruits offering). Giving a first fruits offering requires faith, and Abel demonstrated this faith, which was apparently pleasing to the Lord. As the writer of Hebrews recorded, *"By faith Abel offered God a better sacrifice than Cain did. By faith he was commended as a righteous man, when God spoke well of his offerings" (Hebrews 11:4, NIV).* "By faith" means by the activated Word and with deliberate obedience to follow the law, truth and instruction of God. Through faith, Abel offered a better sacrifice. From his offering he obtained witness as a righteous man. "Righteous" in the Greek means justice (the principle, a decision or its execution). In other words, a man who made a decision by principle, and executed it, then obtained witness as righteous. You don't know you will make and execute the right decisions until you are put to the test!

Hebrews goes on to say that, *"Without faith it is impossible to please God, because anyone who comes to him must believe that he exists and that he rewards those who earnestly seek him" (Hebrews 11:6).* The first fruits offering is based on faith: faith in the fact that the root governs the rest…faith that giving God the whole of the first sets the course for blessings to be released on the rest…faith that God is a rewarder of those who earnestly seek Him.

It was said of Abraham that he believed God. That

faith was credited to him as righteousness, or right standing with God (see Genesis 15:6). Paul expounds on this further in Romans 4:18-22. In the Amplified version it says:

> "[For Abraham, human reason for] hope being gone, hoped in faith that he should become the father of many nations, as he had been promised, 'So [numberless] shall your descendants be.' He did not weaken in faith when he considered the [utter] impotence of his own body, which was as good as dead because he was about a hundred years old, or [when he considered] the barrenness of Sarah's [deadened] womb.
>
> "No unbelief or distrust made him waver (doubtingly question) concerning the promise of God, but he grew strong and was empowered by faith as he gave praise and glory to God, fully satisfied and assured that God was able and mighty to keep His word and to do what He had promised.
>
> "That is why his faith was credited to him as righteousness (right standing with God)."

So, going by what was said of Abraham, it is clear that the faith Abel demonstrated in preparing a first fruits offering is what pleased the Lord, and was also credited to him as righteousness, as we see in Hebrews 11:4. What does righteous mean? It doesn't mean that he was simply a good man, or that he was handsome, or charismatic in his personality. It means Abel was in right standing with God. It means Abel placed God first, in the right place. Abel followed the pattern. He brought a first fruits offering—and because of his faith in that act of worship and acknowledging that it was not by his own hand that he was prosperous in raising sheep, but by God's hand that he was blessed, he was counted as a righteous or just man. When Abel offered to the Lord and it pleased God, Cain got mad. These are times when your obedience to the instruction and Word of God will irritate those in opposition to it.

CAIN'S OFFERING

Once again I say it is not that we are doing something wrong, but that we are not doing enough of what is right. Did Cain bring an offering? Yes, he brought "of the fruit of the ground an offering" to give the Lord. But it was a partial offering.

First of all, without the shedding of blood there is no forgiveness of sins (see Hebrews 9:22). Abel's offering involved bloodshed, but Cain's offering was from the cursed ground (see Genesis 3:17). A first fruits offering is not a sin offering, but coming before God as he did, it was as if Cain was presenting his offering based on his own worthiness, rather than by God's mercy. He presented the work of his own toil, of his own hands, no doubt bringing choice fruits for his offering. As stated earlier, most believe he may have brought fine flour, frankincense and olive oil common for a general gratitude offering, or even a tithe—but not first fruits; *"And whatsoever is first ripe in the land, which they shall bring unto the Lord..." (Numbers 18:13).* Because he gave only a part and not in faith, God was not pleased, or another way to say pleased is "in alignment with."

I can imagine Cain coming with his offering, one that he probably took great pride in preparing and working to arrange. As it was in the Old Testament, when God accepted an offering that was laid upon the altar, He consumed it with fire from heaven. Imagine the feeling of seeing your brother's messy, bloody pile of fat portions from slaughtered lambs lying there next to the bodies of the lambs themselves! Then imagine God consuming that messy offering with fire while your beautiful arrangement lay untouched. The burning fat and meat was a sweet aroma to God, but it was the smell of death to Cain as his offering was unaccepted. Since God has no partiality or respect to people, Cain had to have some knowledge or understanding of what God required and desired.

The Bible says Cain's countenance fell. His face began to reveal what was in his heart—disgust, disappointment and anger that his labor had been for nothing or that doing it "his own way" was not enough. This must have intensified in the days, and weeks, and possibly months to come, as he began to observe the blessings of God manifesting in his brother Abel's life, while Cain continued to toil with the soil. God in His mercy and grace said to Cain, "If thou doest well." To "do well" means to retrace his steps, to consider his ways, to find where he was wrong and then amend his offering and his intention accordingly. What grace and mercy we see in God towards us from the very beginning. Although he was given the opportunity, Cain did not act on divine counsel. The results were devastating.

When Cain violated God's principle, four things happened:

- He lost the presence of God. He was expelled from the presence of God. When you start violating or rebelling against His principles, you will not see the manifested presence of God. Then you have to struggle and strive in your carnality. Life becomes hard because it is the presence of God that brings an ease and flow to life with His provision and favor.

- He lost his connection with his family. His relationships went sour without the presence and protection of God.

- Cain lost his security and his fixed position. He had to flee from his place. He had no secure residence, no covering or safety for his life.

- He lost his harvest. The ground was cursed so it was not to yield any adequate recompense for his tillage. When you violate God's principles, you

<u>lose your blessings</u> and harvest from your labor.

On the other hand, when you abide by God's principles, there are rewards. Hebrews 11:4 says, "Abel was counted as righteous before God." He made a decision by principle with execution. You can determine your future outcomes to a great degree by your decisions. By aligning your life with the Word of God you will reap His wonderful and divine reward.

THE RIGHT PATTERN

Cain worshiped God according to what he thought was enough. His worship had a "form of godliness" but denied "the power thereof" (see 2 Timothy 3:5). In other words, it "looked good" but he failed to tap into the power of the blessing through the power of complete and total faith in God.

We often think we can come and worship God in our own way. Many times we think, "We are doing enough. We show up every Sunday and put our tithe in the offering plate!" Are we supposed to worship God according to the dictates of our own thoughts and imaginations, or according to the patterns and principles that He has established?

It is interesting that the first offering of this kind is found in Genesis. Think about what happened in the Garden of Eden. *"And the LORD God made all kinds of trees grow out of the ground—trees that were pleasing to the eye and good for food. In the middle of the garden were the tree of life and the tree of the knowledge of good and evil"*

111

(Genesis 2:9, NIV). God told Adam that he could eat from any other tree in the garden, but *"you must not eat from the tree of the knowledge of good and evil, for when you eat of it you will surely die" (v. 17)*.

Eve told the serpent that God said not to "touch it" or they would "surely die." She knew what God said, but after the enemy twisted the Word of God a little and convoluted it, notice what happens: *"When the woman saw that the fruit of the tree was good for food and pleasing to the eye, and also desirable for gaining wisdom, she took some and ate it" (Genesis 3:6 NIV)*. How many times do we look at our "firsts" or things that God says belong to Him and decide it is good for us—it is good for food or to buy what we want…it is nice to look at for our own use…and so on? It's not that we are "bad people" who don't love God. We, like Eve are tempted to touch what is an untouchable. In doing so, it will "surely" bring death rather than abundance to our lives. In our "natural" minds, we often do not discern the methods and reasoning of God. The reality is most of God's ways are illogical to our human reasoning. So we end up "compromising" the commands of God. God never calls us to understand Him, but simply to obey Him!

As time passed, Cain became very jealous of the prosperity and of the blessing of the Lord on Abel's life. Seeing Cain's condition, God spoke directly to him, giving him another chance: *"Then the LORD said to Cain, 'Why are you angry? Why is your face downcast? If you do what is right, will you not be accepted? But if you do not do what is right, sin is crouching at your door; it desires to have you, but you must master it'" (Genesis 4:6-7, NIV).*

God gave Cain the opportunity to follow the pattern of what was right; the pattern demonstrated by his brother Abel whose first fruits offering was given in faith. If Cain did what was right his offering would be accepted. Sadly, instead of humbling himself and being taught of the Lord, he developed an unteachable spirit, and in turning from God he opened the door to sin. The word "sin" here mans an offense and its penalty . . . it means to "miss" by inference, to forfeit, lack or lead astray. Like Saul, Cain chose to disobey God, thereby opening the door to demonic influence and out of control behavior which eventually drove him to kill his innocent brother.

Jude refers to this tragedy later on, in warning against those who are apostate, saying, *"Woe to them! They have taken the way of Cain; they have rushed for profit into Balaam's error; they have been destroyed in Korah's rebellion" (Jude 1:11, NIV).* John also warns us to *"not be like Cain who [took his nature and got his motivation] from the evil one and slew his brother. And why did he slay him? Because his deeds (activities, works) were wicked and malicious and his brother's were righteous (virtuous)" (1 John 3:12, AMP).*

BEWARE OF THE "CAIN SPIRIT"

Let us not deceive ourselves. We are all capable of operating in the "Cain spirit." It is a matter of either walking in our carnal nature and fulfilling the desires thereof, or putting God first in everything and walking according to the Spirit of God, and fulfilling His desires.

It is a daily decision that we must make to "take up His cross" and follow Him (Matthew 16:24).

What we call the "Early church" began on the day of Pentecost, when the Holy Spirit was poured out in such a mighty way, as Joel had prophesied. When other Jews who were gathered in the city saw these people baptized in the Spirit, they thought they were drunk. This prompted Peter's powerful address to the crowd, drawing all to repentance. Acts 2:41 notes, *"Those who accepted his message were baptized, and about three thousand were added to their number that day" (NIV)*.

It is in the following verses that we see why those who were part of the Early church had such tremendous power:

> *"They devoted themselves to the apostles' teaching and to the fellowship, to the breaking of bread and to prayer. Everyone was filled with awe, and many wonders and miraculous signs were done by the apostles. All the believers were together and had everything in common. Selling their possessions and goods, they gave to anyone as he had need. Every day they continued to meet together in the temple courts. They broke bread in their homes and ate together with glad and sincere hearts, praising God and enjoying the favor of all the people. And the Lord added to their number daily those who were being saved" (Acts 2:42-47, NIV)*.

They operated in unity, consecration and dedication according to the Spirit, not the carnal nature, and there was life in abundance! During His time of ministry on the earth, Jesus healed the sick, cast out demons and raised the dead, and told us that we—His disciples—would do even greater things. In the Early church there was such a great pouring out and provision that even Peter's shadow falling on a sick person resulted in healing (Acts 5:15)! Hebrews 13:8 declares, *"Jesus Christ the same yesterday, and today and forever."* That same power and provision is available for us today to carry forth the plan and purpose of God in the earth. God will always have a remnant who are equipped and sent forth as agents of assignment to build and advance His Kingdom.

A significant observation to note is that they gave freely to those who had need, and had sold their possessions so that they had all things common.

> *All the believers were one in heart and mind. No one claimed that any of his possessions was his own, but they shared everything they had. With great power the apostles continued to testify to the resurrection of the Lord Jesus, and much grace was upon them all. There were no needy persons among them. For from time to time those who owned lands or houses sold them, brought the money from the sales and put it at the apostles' feet, and it was distributed to anyone as he had need.*

(Acts 4:32-35, NIV).

They shared all things equally for the good of the whole and for the establishment of God's Kingdom. That was their utmost priority. That was their "first fruits" and their blessings were abundant. Let us pay careful attention and recognize that the principles of God do not change. We often fail to embrace the essence of the actions we read of in Scripture against our "modern day" lifestyle and culture. However, the "heroes" of faith we read about had intense degrees of difficulties, challenges, opposition and fears they had to face just as we do. The same power and provision of God is available for us today as we fully commit, obey and dedicate ourselves to God and His Word. And just as the early church, we will also face temptation, persecution and distraction.

Then entered the Cain spirit; that spirit which says, "I can do it my way…I can worship God in a way that makes sense to me and still be blessed." I believe Luke, the writer of the book of Acts, must have been rather amazed by what he saw next. As he wrote to Theophilus in Acts chapter 5: *"Now a man named Ananias, together with his wife Sapphira, also sold a piece of property. With his wife's full knowledge he kept back part of the money for himself, but brought the rest and put it at the apostles' feet" (v. 1, 2).*

That seems fair enough, right? The man wanted to look after his own needs for the future. Since the whole group was being so blessed, he probably got way more for his property than he expected to receive. So…who would know the difference? Certainly not that ex-fisherman-turned-apostle Peter, right? What does he know? Would it really matter?

As Ananias laid his partial gift at Peter's feet, Peter said,

> *"Ananias, how is it that Satan has so filled your heart that you have lied to the Holy Spirit and have kept for yourself some of the money you received for the land? Didn't it belong to you before it was sold? And after it was sold, wasn't the money at your disposal? What made you think of doing such a thing? You have not lied to men but to God." When Ananias heard this, he fell down and died (Acts 5:3-5, NIV).*

Ananias didn't count on the Holy Spirit speaking to Peter. Moments later, when Sapphira walked in, she too dropped dead at hearing Peter's words and her body was carried out. The principle is that when you touch or take something that belongs to God, it can cause death somewhere in your life. God is a life-giver! He wants the absolute best for you! He is not out to harm or hurt you by any means! He is a good God with great promise for you! However, we cannot ignore the "balance" of Scripture. *"Behold, I set before you this day a blessing and a curse. A blessing, if ye obey the commandments of the Lord your God, which I command you this day. And a curse, if ye will not obey the commandments of the Lord your God, but turn aside out of the way which I command you this day, to go after other gods, which ye have not known" (Deuteronomy 11:26:28).*

The Early Church had power because they did things by the pattern of God. They did it the way God instructed. They had unity and they had things in their right order, first things first. They kept the Main Thing—the main thing! Was there provision? Yes. Did they ever lack anything? Never. Jesus at one point sent His disciples out with nothing, yet they had everything they needed by relying on Him. They understood God's power and they understood and obeyed the pattern and instruction of God.

It seems cruel that those two were killed in such a manner after giving—I mean, they did give. But like Cain, they gave what they thought would be right—what's worse, they lied about the rest. Everyone else was giving of the whole, but they withheld and said it was the whole. Remember, one of the reasons for lack that I explained earlier was withholding, and Ananias and his wife quickly lacked life!

They touched what was holy. They indicated that they were giving a first thing, a first fruit, which the Lord claims as His own. But they did not. When you live spiritually minded—following God's pattern, there is life. On the contrary, when you live carnally minded, touching things that are holy, there is death.

NO CONDEMNATION

"There is therefore now no condemnation to them which are in Christ Jesus, who walk not after the flesh, but after the Spirit" (Romans 8:1). I am not sharing these examples to bring condemnation, but to bring clarity. God does not

want you to live in guilt, shame or punishment! He has provided through His Son Jesus complete redemption and freedom for every area of your life! God is serious about first things. Life abundant or lack abundant—the choice is really ours to make. I want you to become positioned to receive the blessings of God so that you may "be a blessing," learning to distinguish the difference between merely giving an offering of what "seems good at the time," and the power that giving the first fruits offering will release in your life and keeping the presence of God as your priority. God knows what's best for us. He wants to bless you—to give you the power and anointing to get wealth, health and wholeness—to establish His covenant. We are redeemed and set free through the blood of Jesus, but the principle that the root establishes the rest is still in effect. This is why first fruits is so vital and key for you to understand and activate in your life. The root establishes or governs the rest. First fruits is the whole of the first, and God sees that as "holy." What you do with all "firsts" governs what occurs with the rest.

I am thankful God gives second chances! Like Cain, God gives us the space and prompting to examine our hearts "and do well." God's promises are not given on the basis of any "good works" we do. The first fruits offering is not about positioning ourselves to "win" God's acceptance and favor. It is about positioning ourselves to honor God and "release" God's blessings—acting in faith in order to see them manifest in our lives. It is your faith in Him that brings God's promises to you.

Chapter 7
One Step of Faith. . .
A Giant Leap in God

As you begin walking out God's principle of first fruits, armed with the revelation and motivation, you may not even be able to comprehend where God will lead you. When David was only a shepherd of his father's sheep, he was promised a kingdom. When he was still hiding and running for his life from King Saul, he was promised victory. It is little wonder how he could praise God with words like, *"My eyes stay open through the watches of the night, that I may meditate on your promises" (Psalm 119:148, NIV).*

David knew how to trust God and keep the Main Thing, the main thing. Even when he was in the desert of Judah, with no place to lay his head, no food and no water, his heart cried out in thirst for God above all else (see Psalm 63:1).

God's promises are not manifested on the basis of any good works you or I have done, or can do but by His grace and kindness to us. The principle of the first fruits offering is about honoring and reverencing God. As you do, you act in faith, which positions you to see those promises manifest in your life. It is your faith in Him that releases God's promises to you. Faith is what empowers you to obtain all that God has promised you. When you keep first things first and give God your first fruits in every area, you align yourself with His plan and see His purposes revealed. But that first step relies on your faith. And it was in faith that I responded to the first promptings of the Holy Spirit to give a first fruits offering.

I am still amazed by the way God began to reveal this powerful principle in my life. It wasn't through a sudden and divine "impartation" of revelation. He led me into the knowledge of first fruits step by step as I responded in faith and obedience. I believe the Lord wanted me to truly get an understanding of first fruits on a practical level, so He actually prompted me to give first fruits before I fully realized what I was doing. Like many revelations that have transformed my life, it has been a progression, more than a "suddenly."

Without Walls International Church began with our family reaching out to the indigent by feeding the hungry, clothing those in need, and reaching out to the community with the Word and practical help. Some of the people we worked with had begun to call us their pastors. Through God's favor, a man gave us use of a small office space on Manhattan Avenue in Tampa. It was very tiny, but it was a start. A handful of faith-filled people wallpapered and painted and got it set up for Bible studies and outreach.

Just after getting our little storefront office/church arranged, I received an unusual request. I was invited to speak about evangelism and outreach by a Greek Orthodox Church in the area. It was a wonderful opportunity, that was very humbling, to consider me to actually "speak." We saw God do wonderful things and many precious people in that church who had a heart for reaching their community got some practical insight on effective outreach.

God supernaturally sustained us through some very humble and meager beginnings. Though we had started a small ministry, we weren't taking any income from it for ourselves, so we had very little on which to live. When I was given a $200 honorarium for speaking at the Greek

Orthodox Church that night, I was ecstatic. It was a tremendous blessing. As I like to put it, I got a "vision" that we were finally going to have hamburger for our "Helper" and cheese for our "Macaroni." At that time, being given $200 was like having $2 million.

One evening that same week, I decided to attend a service at a local church in Tampa to be refreshed and receive the Word. That same night they had a guest speaker. I had just received the $200 check that I was still "basking" in the goodness and awe of the provision of God! At one point during his message, the guest speaker said, "God is speaking to someone here tonight to give it all." I didn't respond. I just put my head down thinking that $200 was our all, and that surely this moment would pass. Then he said it again. It was as if God was standing right in front of me saying, "What are you going to do?"

All is all…whether you are speaking of $200 or $2 million. Letting go of your all, whether it is $200 or $2,000, is still a sacrifice. It is when you "feel" the sacrifice of giving when released. But I gave that sacrificial seed gift of $200 that night, "my all," trusting God to sustain and bless us. I have to admit, as I left the service that night, I thought, "There goes our cheese for our macaroni…man, they got us." Sometimes it is hard not to waiver a little between faith and doubt, but I had learned to be obedient and soft-hearted when the Lord spoke to my heart, so I comforted myself that I had indeed given in faith. Even though I had faith and was obedient, I still "felt" the "price" of sacrificing.

A 5´ 2˝ MESSENGER

The next day, the door opened suddenly at our little office/church. I looked up to see a lady with red hair, standing at about 5'2" tall, approaching. She walked with purpose, and a little bit of an attitude. I wasn't sure what to expect. She walked in and threw down an envelope and said, "God kept me up all night last night. Here... take it." She abruptly turned and walked out the same way she came in. Inside the envelope was a check for $10,000. I could hardly believe it! To be handed that amount of money the day after "giving it all" with that $200 offering was amazing. Of course, my faith was "leaping" then...it was much easier to stand in the position of hearing and obeying God once the results had manifested. But it didn't stop there.

About two hours later, while I was still astounded and in deep gratitude to the Lord over that incredible gift from Him...the same lady came back again. With the same attitude with which she delivered the first gift, she handed over another envelope and said, "Here. God said to give it all," and with that, she turned and marched right back out of the door. That envelope contained a check for $5000! With that $15,000 offering we rented the auditorium of a nearby high school, and began the first services of Without Walls International Church, a ministry reaching many lives for the glory of God.

Prior to moving to Tampa, we gave just about everything we had. When we started the ministry, we gave our all. What I didn't realize was, God had taught me the power in the principle of first fruiting, before I even fully realized what we were doing. I simply knew to be obedient to what He was saying to my heart, and if He said give it all, I obeyed, even though it wasn't easy. In the next few chapters I am going to teach you the important principals of how God sees things, His order and the law of firsts. You will see how, without me fully comprehending the law, the Word still worked in my life when activated.

AN INCREDIBLE DEAL

On a mission to find a permanent place we could establish for God, several of us went out to "spy out the land" looking for other opportunities. I went to an area of town that was not the "booming" or "up and coming" area. The specific location I was focusing on was run down and unused. In fact, it was the old stadium area, and at the time there was nothing to indicate life or prosperity. As I drove by, I saw one particular old brick building sitting off in the back. When I drove up to it I could see that it had been boarded up for some time. It had also been vandalized and had weeds growing up everywhere. But something else happened when I pulled up on that abandoned and distressed property. God clearly impressed to my heart saying, "This is your building." That word was enough for me.

The property appraised for close to $4 million. That was way out of our $500,000 league—and even that would have required a lot of chicken-dinner fundraisers and applying for a loan. But if God said it was ours, we would make an offer. The owners laughed at our offer of $1.2 million.

A few weeks passed, and I still felt as strongly as ever that the property was to be ours. Somewhat reluctantly, but believing God's word, we called and checked on it again. This time, we discovered that the property had been sold in a bulk auction! A bank in Atlanta had purchased most of the distressed properties in that area. But instead of allowing discouragement to take hold, we pressed in with even more determination, expecting God to turn what seemed to be a negative into a positive.

We were warned ahead of time that we'd never get through to the man in charge of the particular property we wanted, especially since it was sold in bulk. But they obviously didn't calculate the one factor that makes all the difference: God's favor. We got directly through to that man, and what's more, he happened to have the deed and the paperwork for that property lying on his desk when we called. When we told him we were interested, he said, "Make me an offer." Now, in the natural, when you've already been turned down—and laughed at—for offering 1.2 million on a property valued at nearly $4 million, your instinct is to go a little higher. But not when God is involved!

We offered $600,000.

The man replied, "Done—but it has to be a cash-only deal, and you have 30 days."

Delighted and rejoicing over God's goodness, we agreed. We took all the money that we had in the bank, which was only about $100,000, and put it into escrow.

127

FOR THOSE WITH BLINDED EYES

When Nicodemus, a Pharisee and a member of the Jewish ruling council, came privately to speak with the Lord, Jesus told him, *"I tell you the truth, no one can see the kingdom of God unless he is born again" (John 3:3, NIV).* The Bible says except a man be born again, he cannot *see.* The Greek word used there for "see" means "to comprehend, understand and have revelation." The moment an unbeliever accepts Jesus as his or her Lord and Savior, he or she begins to see and begins to understand kingdom things. Someone who is not born again will never be able to see or function in God's ways or His Kingdom.

Nicodemus was shocked by the Lord's statement and didn't understand. Jesus pointed out that Nicodemus was one of Israel's teachers, yet he did not understand the kingdom of God. Then Jesus told him, *"I tell you the truth, we speak of what we know, and we testify to what we have seen, but still you people do not accept our testimony" (John 3:10-11, NIV).*

That's why there is no reason to argue with your unsaved friends and relatives over things like bringing your tithes to the storehouse, forsaking not the assembling together (attending church), keeping the Commandments of God or honoring your relationship with Him through obedience to His Word. They don't "get it." You can tell them what you have seen and know, but they will not understand why you come to church every week, pray, fast, tithe or stay faithful to the Lord with no "apparent" reward—at least in their eyes.

Sadly, they cannot understand it because their eyes have not been opened. *"The god of this age has blinded the minds of unbelievers, so that they cannot see the light of the gospel of the glory of Christ, who is the image of God" (2 Corinthians 4:4, NIV).* Unless a person is born again, they cannot comprehend, see or have revelation of the way God does things or "His system of operation." His ways often appear illogical. His methods can look like "madness" to a "natural" mind. The way to experience God's supernatural promises is threefold —by believing, receiving and walking in what God has said. The Bible says in Hebrews 6:12 that the promises of God are inherited through patience and faith. Patience produces the promises of God through your faith, through the Word of God working on the inside of you. Faith takes created tension to function. Remember, the way in which God does things is very different from man. The pressure from the problem is often the activator for faith to flourish. It is a concept that is hard to understand for someone who is not actively living in God's Word.

The best way to share God's principles with those around you is to be a living, breathing example of His Word. When you walk in His ways and are blessed with His presence in your life, others will see a living testimony of God's goodness. You are the sermon that He writes for others to read.

Since we were only a young ministry there was no way we were going to get a loan, and we had no idea how to achieve that without conventional methods of banking. So naturally, we began to fast and pray.

Approximately 18 days later, a woman who had heard about the situation called us. We do not know how she knew all the details. She was not even a member of our church, and we had only met her once before that. But she said, "How much do you need, four...five...six hundred thousand? Ok." And that was the end of the conversation.

As the 30th day drew closer and closer, we continued to do everything we could—fundraising, fasting, marching, you name it. God gave us a specific word out of Psalm 121:3, *"He will not allow your foot to slip or to be moved; He Who keeps you will not slumber" (NIV).* We were encouraged to stand, and it would come to pass.

On day 29, the day before the closing was scheduled, the bank contacted us, concerned the deal would not go through. When the bank representative asked why the money was not yet in escrow, we said, "keep the closing for the scheduled time!" We had a supernatural peace and word from God that all was taken care of!

The next day, before the closing, that same woman who contacted us around the 18th day, called to find out where and when the closing was to take place. When the closing time came, we made our way to the office, still not knowing how it was all going to come together, but keeping faith in what God said. The woman was at the closing with a check for $630,000—enough to cover the entire purchase price as well as the closing costs!

The blessings of that property continue to multiply to this day in so many ways. Multitudes of lives have been changed for the glory of God!

GIVING IT ALL

Walking out the principles of first fruits didn't end with those first lessons. Several years after we started Without Walls, I was in Hawaii teaching and training about outreach, and God stirred my heart, always with His vision for souls and reaching lives with the good news of the gospel at the forefront. I knew He was telling me, "Now is the time to launch TV ministry." What is funny about that is, there was nothing external or internal that would make someone say, "TV ministry is a natural fit for

Paula." Anyone who worked with me back in those days knows how many times we had to retake me just trying to say "God bless you" in front of a camera. It was horrible. I had no natural ability. No confidence. No resource or training to pull from. I had nothing but a rhema word from God that said it would be so.

Without Walls had grown by the grace of God reaching many souls for His kingdom. I knew there was just no way to take on another big expense or project at that time. But in faith and obedience I was willing to go for it.

Soon after that decision, I attended a large ministry conference in Texas. The ministry time took a somewhat unusual turn one evening. I had not seen the leader of the conference do what he did that night under the prompting of the Holy Spirit. Near the end of the service, he began to receive an offering. But it was more like a divine move of God, an act of true worship. There was a marvelous atmosphere in the place. In his directions for the offering, he said God was speaking to some to give $25,000, some to give $15,000, and so on, all the way down to $500, $100 and $50. It was very unusual for this particular ministry and it was very holy.

Now, since I am in covenant with this man of God, I sow regularly into his ministry. During the offering, I felt God prompting me to "give it all," which was my entire savings I had accumulated over the years, in a $25,000 gift. This was significant . . . a large step of faith! It had taken years to save that amount of discretionary income! So I began to think of the large gifts we had already given, and in my own mind worked it out that if I gave $5,000 that night, combined with other offerings we had sown previously, that would make the $25,000. Sometimes we try to maneuver God's Word in an attempt to justify our own desire. That was what I was trying to do. But that wasn't what God meant. I wrote out the check for $5,000 and started to move forward in giving it when I felt a hesitation . . . an internal debate, knowing I was trying to fit obedience to God within the comfort of my framework.

As I continued to debate over what I felt God had already said in my spirit, I literally began to feel my calling—the vision God had given me and said, "It is time,"—beginning to mutate and become crippled within me. God was allowing me to see how my disobedience was causing death to the vision and call of God on my life. It literally jolted me, and I sensed the Lord saying to me, "I asked you to give it all."

So, in faith I gave the entire $25,000 offering God had commanded without compromise or justification. It was a true sacrifice and a true first fruits offering—a giving of it "all" unto the Lord, in obedience to Him. Within days, unexpected and without seeking it out, I received a phone call that would launch the international media ministry now known as Paula White Ministries.

Doors just began to open supernaturally over the next five years. God's favor allowed this ministry to develop in that short period of time what would normally take 20-plus years to do. I didn't know you were supposed to have capital of a million dollars or more in the bank when you started a TV ministry or a partner base and the appropriate equipment. We started it with nothing but a promise from God, one camera, some rent-to-own furniture, one secretary that typed about 23 words per minute, six rotary-dial phones and one computer!

In the natural, there was no way of launching or surviving in that arena. But God's favor makes a way. And His favor was unleashed in abundance because of our willingness to obey and trust Him and to actively demonstrate that trust by giving first fruits. In hind site, I now clearly see the foundation for every promise God had shown us as part of His purpose in our lives and calling, was built from first fruits. When you honor God first, everything else falls into place!

ONE STEP AT A TIME

My life has become a "favor walk" by the grace and goodness of God since learning to apply the principle of first fruits, putting God first in all things. I have not walked out the "traditional" methods of building a career or advancing in a particular field. I have not tried to "open" any particular doors to get "ahead"! Not that I think it is wrong to be pro-active and aggressive with building your dream. My journey has been quite "unorthodox." I have simply followed the flow of His favor that has manifested, proving His covenant. Favor is undeserved access. It takes you places you may not be qualified to go otherwise. Only the favor of God can get you there.

Once I started Paula White Media Ministries, favor opened doors with several secular and Christian networks for specific appearances. Along the way I was told many times there was no way I would ever get on a large Christian network—so I didn't even try. I was not pursuing that option at all. But remember, our media ministry was birthed out of a first fruits offering. God's blessings were released and His favor was hedging us in. I believe that is why I received a phone call one day from a representative of that network. He was calling to inform me that the owner had been trying to make contact because they wanted to offer me a full program slot. A very close person within the network confirmed later that it was truly favor, because that just does not happen!

I often quote the scripture, *"Blessed be the Lord, who daily loadeth us with benefits, even the God of our salvation" (Psalm 68:19).* But I can't tell you how many people have said to me, "Paula, do you really believe that scripture you quote?" Yes, I do! I believe God for daily benefits to be loaded up in my life. Why? Because it has nothing at all to do with me. By faith I am positioned in right standing with God and in the order of God to fulfill the purpose of God in the earth. Our ministry was birthed with first fruits, and the favor of the Lord has never lifted. There have been seasons of "soaring" as well as times of hardship, difficulties and distress. In it all, God has been faithful! I never walked out the principle of first fruits because I wanted "blessing." I did it because I wanted God and His presence in my life. My love and gratefulness for Him was my motivation for following and obeying His instructions. However, I have found that applied principles from His Word will bring His promises and results. It may not be when, where or how you think it should be. But it will always be as He knows and determines it to be! And it can for you, too. It begins with that first step. Take a step of faith and of trust and walk into God's arms of provision for your unique destiny!

Chapter 8
First Results

One of the blessings of sharing God's patterns and principles with believers is seeing how God works miraculously in the lives of those who obey His commands. In Revelation, John wrote about the power of testimonies to defeat the enemy, *"And they overcame him by the blood of the Lamb and by the word of their testimony, and they did not love their lives to the death" (Revelation 12:11, NKJV).*

I believe by sharing some of the awesome things God has done in the lives of others who joined me by putting God first and in giving the offering of first fruits, you will be encouraged and empowered to put first things first in your own life,

People from all different situations and walks of life have overcome lack and defeat by exercising their faith in God, prioritizing His presence and giving first fruits offerings. I stress that there is no "magical formula" or "manipulation tactics" that guarantee you some false hope and promise but leave you disillusioned and disappointed. First fruits is ALL about First things First . . . that is, prioritizing His presence in your everyday life. God is the One Who is the Rewarder of our obedience. May you rejoice and be blessed to see His faithfulness in the lives of so many!

Here are just a few testimonies from those who have put God's Word to the test and seen "first results."

We received a hand-written note from a man who had been separated from his wife for nearly two years. He writes, "Last January I gave my first fruits offering for the very first time. The devil fought me every step of the way in making my decision, but I decided to listen to the voice of God instead and I offered my first week's pay."

Notice the incredible blessings that were released in his life over the course of that same year. He continues, "I saw my income increase $20,000 after I received a promotion, my wife and I have reconciled after being apart for two years, my wife's health has been restored, we have purchased a new home, and God has been blessing other members of our family as well."

I love how moved this man was by the overflowing abundance of the blessings of God in his life. He concludes his letter, "God has been so good that, even as I write this letter, tears of joy are coming down my face. To God be the glory."

The enemy had stolen from this man's life on many sides, but after his first fruits offering, his entire situation turned around. Instead of leaving the door open for the enemy, he received promotion...reconciliation... healing...land and more!

RIPPLES ON THE POND

One dear woman wrote to us recently that she had never heard of first fruits before hearing me teach the principle on our program. She says, "I was really excited and went online and printed the teaching. That evening I shared it with my husband. He had just received his two-week paycheck and said, 'I believe we need to do this.' He gave that entire check as a first fruits offering. The next week he received a check from someone who said she didn't know why she sent it...she just knew that she should! The next week I took my one-week paycheck and my tithe and gave it to my pastor—with the explanation that it was a first fruits offering. He was overwhelmed. I said, 'This is something God has told us to do.' The ripples on the pond are going out!

This woman had the opportunity to share a life-giving principle with the man of God appointed to her congregation, and he was able to pronounce the blessing or benediction over her household. But notice that this is not a one-time blessing. It doesn't mean that you're blessed for a day or two after you give your first fruits. The testimonies in my own life, and those I read on a regular basis that come from other people tell of blessings that continue far beyond the time of the offering. That is because the priest (or man/woman of God) causes the blessing to rest on your household.

FIRST FRUITS OPENS DOORS

Beverly is a wonderful, faithful woman of God. After serving on the mission field for about four years, she sensed the Lord's direction to return to the states. Beverly relocated to Atlanta, Georgia, intending to live there for about a year. She moved in with a friend for a short time, but quickly went through the $400 she had to get started. Finding a job was imperative. With a background in human resources, she sought something in that field, only to find herself working at a car dealership selling cars instead. But God was with her. Though she had never sold cars before in her life, she became the top salesperson on the floor a short time after she began. Beverly had a few debts from the past, and because she'd been overseas, some of those debts had even gone into collection and creditors were beginning to harass her. Beverly said,

> "I began to think about the fact that, if I was going to spend a year in Georgia, working and living there, I needed to think about sowing seed. So I began to pray and ask God for His guidance. Tithing I understood, but I also knew that, at the beginning of the year, you give a first fruits offering. So after praying to God about this very thing, I saw Paula White talking about first fruits in a televised message. Even though I had not had the opportunity to give a significant first fruits offering for some time because I was not working, I did understand the importance of it. So I asked God if I was to sow into her ministry. December was my best month at the dealership, so my first fruits offering of my first check of the coming year was going to be the best offering I had ever given. I felt the Holy Spirit direct me to sow the seed into Paula White's ministry.
>
> Through my dealings at the local bank, I had come to know the bank manager rather well. She offered me a position at the bank, which I accepted.

I started paying off debts. I realized that the offering I gave was not just to bless me financially. It was an offering that opened doors and gave me insight and understanding. First fruits is one of the hardest things to do, because you are just taking the whole thing and saying 'God, here it is…I trust You to manage it for me,' and He does! It was like God said, 'Because you have entrusted Me with the responsibility for your year, your life and your livelihood, I am going to show you things and make things known to you that are important to your well being.'"

When God gives you revelation, that revelation causes you to move out in faith. When revelation hits your spirit, you don't just sit in the boat and watch everybody else walk on water. You say to yourself, "If they can walk on water, so can I!" Like our father of faith, Abraham, who demonstrates in Romans chapter 4 that he had hope when there seemed to be no hope, you must start calling those things that are not *as though they are*. Start speaking and agreeing with the fact that everything you need has already been provided—all godliness and all spiritual blessings have already been given to you. You just need to walk in it.

OTHER STORIES OF FIRSTS

Putting God first in the morning has changed North Carolinian Wendy's life. She heard the teaching on first fruits and began to practice it. She writes, "I have been spending time every morning with God and have been truly blessed." She also gave her first financial first fruits offering. Just seven days later she received an abundance of groceries—that she could not afford—from people who had no idea how desperate her situation happened to be.

A precious member of our congregation let us know recently how promotion manifested in her life after giving two weeks pay as her first fruits offering in January. On January 30, she was called into the office at her corporate health job and asked if she was interested in receiving a promotion to a higher position than she currently held. She was offered a $4,000 increase in pay starting the following week.

Linda from Texas suffered from hepatitis of the liver for 32 years. She began the year recently by sowing her entire disability check as a first fruits offering. A few months later she went back to her doctor. He said, "I don't know what happened!" They could not find any trace of the virus in her body. This is the second year of giving her first fruits offering.

Anthony from Nassau wrote to tell us how he had seen the teaching on first fruits. Revelation hit his heart—but he truly had no money. Anthony had been unemployed for five months. So he decided to pray. "Lord," he said, "if you want me to give a first fruits offering, you will need to send me the money." Already, Anthony acknowledged that he had no ability to get wealth outside of God's provision—and God did indeed provide. Anthony gave a first fruits offering of $900, an amount he felt would adequately represent one week of pay from a job he did not yet have. His check arrived at our offices on the first of February. We found out later that the very next day, February 2, a gentleman at his church who is a CEO asked Anthony to call him because he had a brand new job for him. But that's not all. The new job paid four times what his first fruits offering represented per month! Anthony now says, "First fruits is awesome!"

Eunice from Texas said that shortly after sending in her sacrificial first fruits offering, she was asked by her boss to bring some folders of work to him. After he received the folders, he told her she was getting a raise of $10,000 more a year! She wrote, "If I had thoughts of it being something I had done, those thoughts left immediately. God confirmed the raise was because of my obedience in first fruits. As I was leaving to go back to my office, my boss made this statement . . . 'Now you can tithe more!' I thanked God for activating His promise and releasing blessings into my life."

Shardohn of Virginia had never heard the scripture found in Romans 11:16 that reads, "If the part of the dough offered as firstfruits is holy, then the whole batch is holy; if the root is holy, so are the branches." But that one scripture opened her eyes to the principle of first fruits this past January. She writes, "I had a financial need for my rent so I was a little nervous about giving first fruits, but I did not let that stop me. I gave my first fruits offering of $1000.00. My faith came by hearing the word of God and God used this opportunity to show off on my behalf. Now I work only three days per week and the Lord has allowed me to make more money than I did when I was full time. Now I get to spend more time with my family. How exciting! Also my real estate business, and other business ventures are beginning to blossom. To God be the Glory. God cannot fail!"

The blessings of God come in so many different forms. Julia wrote to tell us, "Last year my husband and I gave of our first paychecks for a first fruit. During the year, we have been doubly blessed, I gave birth to two beautiful twin girls and my husband has been shown tremendous favor by his boss. I believe all this blessing was due to our faithfulness on giving first fruit. Thank you for being willing to teach on such a controversial subject, we have been blessed because of your faithfulness."

A couple from Pennsylvania were determined to pay off their credit card debts and had established a plan to do so over a 15-month period. After hearing the teaching on first fruits, faith rose up in their hearts, and they knew God would honor their obedience. So they gave their first fruits offering in January, and were able to pay their large credit card debts off in just six months. The wife's name is Paula, and she writes, "We also were able to take two paid-for vacations to spend with family. I was able to attend the Paula White Alive Conference with my girlfriend. We were able to save a small nest egg to have money saved for emergencies in the future. And my husband was given a new job with better pay, and wonderful opportunity for growth and professional development with a financially strong company. It is amazing to see the Lord's blessing beginning to overtake us. We are truly thankful to God for giving us the opportunity to give our first fruits offering!"

Shannon from North Carolina writes, "I have to thank you for your teachings on first fruits. We are avid tithers and give special offerings, however, we had never heard of 'first fruits.' Everything you said was backed up by Scripture. So, we sowed our first fruits offering with the faith and belief that God would use it to His glory, and would bless us. Never in our imagination did we think

I will hear what God the LORD will speak: for he will speak peace unto his people, and to his saints: but let them not turn again to folly. Surely his salvation is nigh them that fear him; that glory may dwell in our land (Psalm 85:8-9, KJV).

He would bless us like He did. My husband just received a huge promotion and his salary was increased almost 30 percent, which is unheard of! We will have to relocate, but we are so excited just thinking about how God is going to use us."

Many of these first fruits offerings—one week and two weeks pay—may seem large. God says that all first fruits belong to Him, great or small. He honors the faith you demonstrate in giving Him the "firsts." Deirdre from Detroit can testify to this fact. She gave all she had—$18.00—to the Lord in a first fruits offering. Six-months later she was running her own mortgage business. Not only that, a few months later God blessed her with office space in downtown Detroit in the heart of the financial district. She had favor with a local radio station, receiving a month of 30-minute radio spots for the price of 30-second spots, with the potential to reach 4 million people. Her national managers were so impressed with her progress, the following year she was asked to meet with the owner of the company. She said, "I never thought that my life would change from earning $18 a week to meeting with a billionaire."

After hurricane Katrina devastated New Orleans, Louisiana, Tammara was among those who lost absolutely everything. She was evacuated to Texas, and began to make her home there. She had received no money from FEMA, and she had no insurance on her Louisiana home or belongings. The only income she received was an unemployment check. She trusted our ministry as a place to give her first fruits offering and gave her unemployment check, a total of $98. Just one week later she received a check for $2,196.

Presenting an offering of one week's salary was truly a sacrifice for Susan in New Mexico. But she understood the principle of faith behind first fruits, and gave her offering to our ministry. She wrote to tell us that she received a new job with an $18,000 a year increase in salary the following March. "God is so faithful," she writes. "I am sowing my first fruits offering again this year. Praise God!"

"Praise the Lord for miracles," begins the letter we received from Janika of Rhode Island. She continued, "As soon as I sent my first fruits offering, I received a phone call from my lawyer. He called to notify me that I had finally received the settlement from my case which had been on hold for over two years." She had lost hope for receiving any money from this case. But the first fruits offering truly opens doors!

Tracy from Texas wrote: "I watched your show and heard you teach on first fruits. I knew that I was not watching your show that day by accident. I decided first fruits would be one week's salary. I got up the courage to discuss it with my husband. He said to do whatever I wanted . . . he just did not think that it was wisdom (I knew better!). I sent our first fruits and within a few days, we got a check in the mail for about $4,700! I know (my husband) does not understand, but one day he will, because I am sowing for things that money cannot buy — for my husband, children, children's children and so on. Thank you for that teaching! The prosperity in my life has nothing to do with money!"

The final testimony I want to share with you is so colorful, and such an example of this very thing. It comes from a woman named Sarah, who lives in Eaton, Colorado. She starts her letter with the statement, "The Lord's timing is always right." Sarah understands that the first fruits offering is about the principle that establishes the pattern of breakthroughs and blessings in your life. She had been looking to purchase land with a house, or a place she could build for some time. She had a large down payment saved in the bank, and had been pre-qualified for a large mortgage loan, but could not find the right place. Then the Lord told her to give her entire down payment as a first fruits offering. That was on the eighth of January.

INVESTING IN KINGDOM WORK

When you bring your first fruits into God's storehouse, it not only blesses you, but also accomplishes the work of God's Kingdom. The Bibles says that, *"Moreover he commanded the people that dwelt in Jerusalem to give the portion of the priests and the Levites, that they might be encouraged in the law of the LORD" (2 Chronicles 31:4, KJV).* Other versions say, *"to give the portion due to the priests and the Levites, that they might devote themselves to the law of the LORD" (NASB).*

The writer of Hebrews said, *"Obey your leaders and submit to their authority. They keep watch over you as men who must give an account. Obey them so that their work will be a joy, not a burden, for that would be of no advantage to you." (Hebrews 13:17, NIV).* The men and women of God whom He has called to preach His Word and watch over His flock are positioned to feed and to watch over your soul. When you give of your first fruits, you are not only helping them continue ministering to you, but you are also sowing into the lives of the lost and hurting.

Jesus warned, *"Do not store up for yourselves treasures on earth, where moth and rust destroy, and where thieves break in and steal. But store up for yourselves treasures in heaven, where moth and rust do not destroy, and where thieves do not break in and steal. For where your treasure is, there your heart will be also" (Matthew 6:19-21, NIV).*

You cannot be connected without treasure. God uses your gifts, your treasure, to connect you in covenant with the ministry. You are drawn to or in covenant with ministries because your heart identifies with the vision of that ministry.

Look at 2 Chronicles 31:4. There was great revival in the land during Hezekiah's reign. The armies of Israel were victorious over their enemies and in destroying the sinful objects and practices of the land. Hezekiah assigned priests and Levites to sing praises and give thanks offerings at the

Temple to honor the Lord. But it also says that *"the king contributed from his own possessions for the morning and evening burnt offerings and for the burnt offerings on the Sabbaths, New Moons and appointed feasts as written in the Law of the LORD"* (2 Chronicles 31:3, NIV).

He then ordered the people to bring the priests and Levites their portion so they could devote themselves to the law of the Lord. Do you know how the people responded? *"Azariah the chief priest, from the family of Zadok, answered, 'Since the people began to bring their contributions to the temple of the LORD, we have had enough to eat and plenty to spare, because the LORD has blessed his people, and this great amount is left over'"* (2 Chronicles 31:10, NIV).

The people gave so joyfully that it was piled up in heaps! Their generosity and faithful giving helped keep the vision alive in the man of God and helped bring to pass all that he was called to do and more. As a result, the people continued to be blessed during Hezekiah's reign. I love how that chapter ends: *"This is what Hezekiah did throughout Judah, doing what was good and right and faithful before the LORD his God. In everything that he undertook in the service of God's temple and in obedience to the law and the commands, he sought his God and worked wholeheartedly. And so he prospered"* (2 Chronicles 31:20-21, NIV).

God blesses and prospers you to be a blessing to others to build and advance His kingdom and establish His purpose. May you always keep the presence of God your priority!

The very next day, her friend was passing through the town of Eaton when she saw a site so peculiar she called Sarah to tell her about it. She said, "A very large squirrel was struggling to cross the road carrying a large ear of yellow corn in his mouth."

Her friend was laughing at this strange sight when she noticed that there was a for sale sign on the 'bed & breakfast' just across the street. Sarah continued, "I had a vision in 1978 about a house the Lord wanted to use for His people." She asked her friend if the house was yellow with a wrap-around porch. It was. She asked if it had a swing on the porch, facing west. It did. She asked if it had a large blue spruce in the front yard. Of course, it did. Sarah became ecstatic.

She went to see the house as soon as she could. Once she laid eyes on it, she knew it was indeed the great Victorian house she had seen in a vision so many years ago. But there was a problem: She'd given her entire down payment as a first fruits offering!

The favor of God allowed her to qualify for a 100% mortgage on the property and she moved in that February. Almost a year later, the Lord told her that someone was coming to pay off the mortgage. Upon receiving that word from the Lord, like the widow of Zarephath acting on the revelation of God's provision, Sarah sowed another offering to see even greater breakthroughs based on God's promise.

The "bed & breakfast" is now called "The Secret Place," and is a place, every second Friday of the month, for Christians from all over Colorado and Nebraska to gather and spend the night. Some drive for hours to be here, and people are healed and delivered. In addition to the outpouring of the Holy Spirit, people enjoy the peace that surpasses understanding at The Secret Place."

You will live in the blessings of God when you

determine to follow His principles. Start now to establish the pattern for your family that the first thing you do on the first day of every week is go to the house of the Lord to honor and worship Him. Set time aside on the Sabbath to study His Word, putting knowledge of His Word in the first place in your life. Seek first His kingdom by giving God the first moments of each day, thereby establishing how the rest of your day will go. Give to God what is His—the first of all things, and the tithe. The first check from a new job, the first of the year's salary, and so on. Your first fruits offering might be a day, it might be a week, it might be a month.

Remember God as first in all things. When you bring your life into alignment with what the Word of God says about you, then you will find the pattern of your life. We see God as being all-powerful, all-wise, all-loving and eternal. But we should also see Him as our Rock among the shifting sands of life. See Him as the Balm of Gilead in the midst of your sickness. See Him as your Provider in the midst of your lack. When you first fruits the Lord, you are positioning yourself for just that! As David wrote, "I said to the LORD, 'You are my Lord; apart from you I have no good thing'" (Psalm 16:2, NIV).

BLESSED FOR A PURPOSE

David also said, "The LORD knoweth the days of the upright: and their inheritance shall be for ever. They shall not be ashamed in the evil time: and in the days of famine they shall be satisfied" (Psalm 37:18-19). We have established that it is the first fruits offering that "gives you the power to get wealth," (Deuteronomy 8:18, NKJV). By putting the Lord in the proper place in your life, you release the promises of His blessings. But those blessings serve a purpose. When we are blessed, God is magnified and establishes His covenant with His people.

In Egypt, the Israelites had gone from an extremely prosperous nation to an oppressed people in slavery after 400 years. Pharaoh had even begun to kill the firstborn Israelite boys in an attempt to dwindle their numbers. They had nothing. But when God delivered His people, *"The Israelites did as Moses instructed and asked the Egyptians for articles of silver and gold and for clothing. The LORD had made the Egyptians favorably disposed toward the people, and they gave them what they asked for; so they plundered the Egyptians" (Exodus 12:35-3, NIV).* He gave them favor and three million Israelites walked out of that rich land with an abundance of gold and valuables. According to Deuteronomy, God blessed them in order to establish His covenant.

Later, as Moses stood in the presence of the Lord receiving specific instructions as to how to use the plunder of gold and silver that they had taken, at the bottom of the mountain the people had decided to use their wealth to fashion an idol of gold that they could worship (see Exodus 32:2-4). That was not God's purpose for blessing His people. God gives us the ability to get wealth for a purpose. I have often said that your money has a mission. Money without purpose is materialism. In my opinion, the greatest purpose of financial prosperity is when you can begin to affect another person's destiny. We are to leave our children with an inheritance. We are to enjoy a portion of the fruit of our labor. The Word of God clearly shows us how to manage and distribute the money with which we have been entrusted. We have a mission to spread the news of His Kingdom, and the gospel of the Lord Jesus. We are stewards over all He has trusted us with.

NOTES

NOTES

NOTES

NOTES

NOTES